ALONG CAME BABY

J. S. COOPER

ABOUT ALONG CAME BABY

I just wanted to have some fun . . .

It all started when I moved into my new apartment in Brooklyn and met my neighbor, Danielle. We became fast friends and so when she had to go out of town on an emergency work trip, I agreed to give her brother her keys so he could look after her dog. And then I met him. Her brother was Carter Stevens, and he was sex on legs. He was a banker by day and a musician by night; arrogant, handsome, with the most tantalizing smile I'd ever seen. When he invited me to his show, I couldn't say no.

He wasn't looking for a relationship . . .

The night of the show we stumbled back to my place and had the kind of fun I can only blush thinking about. I'd never had a one-night stand before, but one night soon led to two, which led to three. Carter was exciting and mysterious, but he was a total playboy. He made it clear that this was some no strings attached fun.

But fate had other plans for us . . .

I thought we'd been careful, but I guess there was that one time that we weren't. And now, I'm pregnant, and Carter Stevens and I have to figure out what to do because one thing we both know for sure is that the baby is coming, and we have no idea what to do next.

Copyright © 2018 by J. S. Cooper
Proofreader: Marla Esposito

❀ Created with Vellum

Join My Mailing List to receive a
FREE BOOK!

For the first musician I ever loved, you are my Carter, and this story is for you.

*L*ila

*I*t all began with two words. Two words that I never thought anyone would say to me. Especially not someone as hunky as Carter Stevens. But hey, I guess you just never know when fate is going to look you in the face and say, hey girl, tonight is your night.

"Hey, sexy." That's what he said. "Hey, *sexy*." And with that I was gone. His tone was warm, his smile was wide, his blue eyes deep, intense, sparkling as they ran up and down my body. His dark blond hair was cut low to his head, and he had a light grazing of facial hair that I wanted to caress with my fingers to see if it was soft or rough.

"Hey," I said, not knowing what else to say. I wanted to say, hey, sexy, are you as good in bed as you look, but I hadn't had that much to drink yet.

"I like that necklace," he said, his hands reaching up

and lightly grazing my neck as he played with the silver necklace my mom had gotten me a few Christmases before from Tiffany's. "Oops," I said as someone hit me from behind and I stumbled forward into him. "Sorry," I said and gave him a small smile as I realized how close his lips were to mine.

"Nothing to be sorry about." He grinned as his hands reached out to my waist to steady me. The bar was packed tonight and there were people surrounding us on all sides, drinking and excited as they listened to the music and chatted. "Thanks for coming tonight, Lila." He leaned forward and whispered in my ear, his breath tickling my eardrum and making my stomach and heart skip a beat.

"No worries, thanks for inviting me," I said as coolly as I could. "This is awesome and I can't wait to see you perform. You play guitar, right?" I asked, wanting to keep the conversation going, but not knowing what else to say. I wanted to tell him to keep his hands on me. I wanted to tell him that we should find a back room somewhere so I could feel his hands all over me and his lips too. If I'd been a bit braver, I would have reached up and kissed him, but I was still feeling a bit shy. He was just so hot and he made me just a little bit nervous.

"And I sing." He nodded. "We're a local band, but we have a lot of support," he said as he looked around and nodded at some guys that were standing near us and waving.

"This is a cool spot. I've never been to Rockwood Music Hall before," I said as I looked around. The stage was directly to our left and the bar just behind us to the right. The venue was pretty small, but it was a well laid out space. I looked up and saw a balcony with seats and saw people standing and dancing to the band on the stage. Everyone seemed like they were having a lot of fun and the feeling was contagious. There was magic in the air and it seemed like everyone here knew it.

"We're going to go on in about ten minutes," he whispered into my ear again, his tongue lightly touching my inner ear. My whole body trembled at the intimacy of his action and my hands moved down to his as they were still on my waist. "I have to go to the back and grab my gear and get ready. However, let's get a drink when I'm done, yeah?" He leaned back and his eyes gazed into mine with a devilish look. The way he stared into my eyes made me think bad thoughts. Really bad thoughts.

"Just a drink?" I said, with a teasing smile, as my fingers ran down his lightly. I wasn't quite sure what had come over me. Maybe it was the two glasses of wine I'd had before I'd come out tonight. Maybe they were finally going to my head. Maybe it was the appreciative gazes he was giving me. Maybe it was the way his fingers pressed into my waist as if they wanted to get to know me better. I don't know what it was, but I was ready to have some fun tonight. No matter what that meant. And I was almost inebriated enough to let him know the thoughts in my head and exactly what I wanted.

"It's never just a drink," he said and winked and then because he knew that he was the sexiest man alive and could get away with anything, he leaned forward and gave me a quick kiss, and his hands then ran down my back to my ass and he pulled me toward him. My body was crushed against his now and he was providing me with warmth and tingles unlike any I'd felt before. "Tonight we're going to make some sweet music, baby," he said against my lips and I gasped as he slid his tongue into my mouth. He tasted like whiskey and though I've never been a huge fan of the taste before, tonight it was like manna on my lips.

"Okay," I whispered back to him as he pulled away, and I watched as he walked away toward the back of the room and through a door. I ran my hands through my hair quickly and searched in my handbag for some mints. I popped one into my mouth and sucked on it, trying to stop the flow of excitement from running through my veins. I licked my lips nervously as I stood there and walked over to the bar to get myself a drink.

There were two guys standing by the bar giving me an appreciative look and I just smiled at them coyly. In any other circumstances, I might have been interested in a little flirtation, but not tonight. Tonight, my eyes were on Carter Stevens and only Carter Stevens. He was sex on legs and I was determined to know if the promises his eyes were making would be fulfilled by the end of the night. I wasn't to know that within a month from tonight I would find out I was pregnant and the last thing I would be thinking about would be him calling me sexy.

"You My Brown Eyed Girl"

I'm what some people would call a true believer. I believe in true love. The kind you read about in fairy tales. I think that somewhere out there my Prince Charming is just waiting to meet me and sweep me off of my feet. He's somewhere out there. Maybe over the rainbow. Maybe in another galaxy. Maybe he's stuck under a rock somewhere. I don't know where he is to be honest, but he sure as hell hasn't come knocking on my door in my lifetime.

Don't get me wrong I've dated some nice guys; or rather guys that seemed nice at first until I realized they weren't. I'm like a jerk magnet. The bigger the jerk, the faster they come running to me. My friends call me Lila Delilah Asshole Caller. I know it doesn't even rhyme, but I couldn't disagree with them. I think my name and phone

5

number got put in the asshole black book or something because they love me. But I haven't given up on finding my true love. Hope springs eternal and all that good stuff. Right now, I'm just taking a little break from dating to concentrate on my career. A career I'm not really sure I'm cut out for, if I'm honest.

I work as a litigation attorney and I hate it. The only thing I like about my job is the paycheck. Who am I to laugh at a six-figures salary? I never thought I'd make this much money in my life, and while the paychecks are great, I'd give the job up in a heartbeat if I didn't have debt up to my eyeballs. It turned out that law school was a costly endeavor and now I have to work a job I hate to pay off a debt that I got just to get the job I hate. Does that even make sense? But I digress, no one cares about my sucky job. We all have sucky jobs. I care more about finding the right man. Well, eventually. Right now, I'm just working my sucky job and swiping on dating apps hoping to get some nice dates with some nice guys. So far, I'm zero for ten. I've been on ten dates in the last six months and all the guys have been awful. I'm about ready to just say forget it and have some fun. I just don't really know who or how to have said fun. I want to get married one day. I want to have kids. I want that picture-perfect family, but I also want it with the right guy. I can picture him in my head. I've just not met him yet.

"Thank you so much Lila." My next-door neighbor Danielle grinned at me as she handed me her spare set of keys and what looked like an expensive bottle of Pinot Noir. "You only have to look after Frosty for two nights and then my brother, Carter, will be by."

"So he'll call me to let me know when he's going to pick up the keys?" I asked as I placed her keys on my small and narrow hallway table. My apartment was very small, but had been updated, and frankly I was lucky that I could even fit in any size hallway table. I kept the bottle of wine in my hand because I was going to open that bad boy as soon as she left, right before I took her golden retriever, Frosty out for a long walk in Prospect Park.

"Yup." She nodded, her blond hair swaying back and forth as she looked at me thoughtfully. "I gave him your number and he'll call you tomorrow, I think." Her blue eyes seemed distant for a few seconds and then she smiled. "Don't worry, he will pick them up at a time available to you. He thinks he's so busy, but I told him that you're doing me a favor so he needs to pick them up at a time convenient for you."

"That's okay." I smiled at her. "He can pick them up here or at my office. So, he's going to come by in the mornings and evenings to walk Frosty?" I asked again, curiously. "I'm sorry I can't commit to taking care of him while you're away, but work is crazy right now and I'm not sure I can get away at the required hours for him to go out." I'd just started my job as an associate at a corporate law firm and the hours were awful. The pay was good, but the hours were long and tedious.

"No worries," Danielle said. "And no, I think he's going to move into my place for the next month." She made a face. "He lives on the Upper West Side, he went to Columbia and so he stayed in the area. And well it's just too much of a commute for him to go back and forth from the UWS to here." She sighed and then shuddered. "I can't imagine what my place is going to look like when I get back. He's such a slob."

"Aw, I'm sorry," I said and laughed. I knew that I had

also been a slob in college as well. I was still pretty untidy now, so I was not one to judge anyone else. "That's nice that he's willing to do that for you, though."

"He's not nice at all. He's only doing it because I'm paying him." She shook her head. "Brothers!"

"Aw," I said again and then looked down at the bottle of wine in my hands. "Want some?"

"I shouldn't," she said slowly and then looked at her watch. "Okay, well maybe I have time for one glass." She stepped into my apartment properly and closed the door behind her. "Thanks, Lila."

"No worries, you brought me the wine. Come on in. I have some cheese and crackers as well. And some brownies."

"I can't have brownies." She patted her slender waist. "I just got back from yoga."

"Aw, okay." I smiled at her and sighed inwardly. I didn't want Danielle to think I was a fat ass, so I'd have to have a brownie after she left. Not that I thought she would judge me terribly, but Danielle was a new friend and I was still trying to make a good impression on her. I'd only moved into this apartment three months ago and she was my first and only friend in the building.

"But hey, who's going to tell my trainer?" She grinned as she settled down on the couch. "Plus I'm going to be in England and it's going to be freezing there. I'll need a couple of extra pounds to keep me warm at night, seeing as I won't have Frosty."

"I guess you'll miss him a lot."

"He's like my baby." She nodded. "But he'll have a lot of fun with Carter. Carter loves to jog so I'm sure Carter will be out all the time."

"That will be good for Frosty," I said with a smile as I opened the bottle of wine. Young college guys were so lucky to have so much time to go jogging. I rarely had any time to do anything now that I was working full time as an associate at a law firm. I'd always wanted to be a lawyer, and I enjoyed my job, for the most part, but I just had to work so damn much. If it wasn't for the very nice pay, I think I definitely would have pursued a different career.

"Yeah, Frosty loves Carter, but then everyone loves Carter." She rolls her eyes. "To say he's a ladies' man is an understatement."

"Oh?" I asked curiously, wondering what her brother looked like.

"Yeah." She took the glass of wine that I handed her. "You know there are some men that can say and do anything and get away with it because they're so good looking and charming?"

"Not personally, but I know the type you mean." I laughed, and we clinked glasses. "Cheers."

"Cheers," she said, and she took a small sip. "My parents even fall under his spell, he can do no wrong."

"Aw," I said again, not really knowing what to say. She wasn't exactly painting her brother in the best light.

"Oh, don't get me wrong." She shook her head and laughed as she sipped some more wine. "I love him. He's an amazing brother. Lots of fun and he's always been here for me." She nodded. "I think I'm just a little bitter because guys seem to just get away with so much."

"I understand, girl, don't worry." I pat her on the shoulder. Danielle and her boyfriend had recently broken up and while they hadn't dated for a tremendously long time, she was still upset. I was pretty sure he had cheated on her or something like that, but she hadn't told too much.

"And I can't believe the office is sending me to England for this project." She rolled her eyes. "Like I was the only one they could think of." She shook her head again. Danielle worked in HR for some hotel chain, and supposedly they needed her to go and help with the staffing for some new hotel chain they'd acquired because half of the staff had quit in the last week.

"I think because we're single women, we're the first ones that are chosen for the not so nice jobs," I said thinking about my own experience at the law firm I worked at. I was on the most boring cases with the most discovery and the longest hours, but I accepted it as paying my dues. "When you get back, we will go and have a fun night out."

"That would be amazing." Danielle's blue eyes lit. "Have I told you how happy I am that you moved in here?"

"Only like a hundred times, so please keep it up." I grinned at her. "And you're not half as happy as I am," I said honestly. Moving into this apartment three months ago had been like a dream come true. I'd finally been able to afford my own place and even though I was decorating it slowly, it was really starting to feel like a home. "I got really lucky moving into this gorgeous place and getting an awesome new neighbor and a friend to boot."

"Aw, you're so sweet, Lila," Danielle said. "Here's to us," she said and raised her glass again.

"Also." She paused, her face looking slightly awkward and nervous for some reason as she looked at me.

"Yeah?" I prodded for her to continue, curious as what she was going to say next.

"So I shouldn't say this and I normally wouldn't but . . ." Her voice trailed off again, and she just shook her head. "My brother, Carter, he's a very charismatic, very good-looking guy and, well, he's a lot of fun, but he's a total playboy."

"Okay?" I laughed. "Why are you telling me this?"

"You're a pretty girl, Lila," she said with a smile. "My brother loves pretty girls. And he loves the chase, so he's going to want you badly. I'm sure of it. Don't give him the time of day. He's a heartbreaker, pure and simple."

"I'll remember that." I grinned at her. "I'm not looking for a relationship or anything right now, so I think we're good."

"I know you've said that before but I figured I'd give you my advanced warning, just in case."

"Thanks, but no need to worry about me. Between work and sleep I have no time for anything else. I'm a regular boring Betty."

"I don't think you're a boring Betty, but just remember what I said. He can be a real charmer when he wants to be and well, I've seen too many friends fall under his spell and then . . ." Her voice trailed off and she made a face. "But let's have one more glass of wine before I have to go. It's going to be a long flight tonight."

"You'll have a great time," I said as I poured her some more wine. "And don't worry about Frosty. I'll make sure to remind Carter to walk him if I see him around the building."

"Thanks, Lila. You're amazing," she said as we clinked glasses one more time and we both took another long sip of the expensive wine she'd brought me.

"Also, you don't have to worry about me, I'm not into college guys." I laughed. "I'm way too old to hang."

"College?" She looked at me with a confused expression. "Oh, he's not in college." She laughed. "Though you'd think he only recently graduated. He's actually slightly older than me. He's thirty-five."

"Oh," I said. "I thought he was a lot younger than that from the way you were talking about him. I'm

11

surprised I've never met him before. He's not come over before?"

"No." She shook her head. "He's a busy guy. He works on Wall Street during the day and he's in some stupid band that plays a lot of local gigs." She rolled her eyes. "He thinks he's some sort of rock god."

"Oh yeah?" I asked curiosity getting the better of me. I loved musicians for some reason. They were just so talented and sexy. Though I wasn't going to tell Danielle that; I'd always imagined having some sort of secret fling with a rock star. I didn't want her to start worrying about me.

"Yeah." She finished up her wine. "We usually get together for lunches during the week because his nights and weekends are packed. I should feel honored he made time to look after Frosty."

"If he's a Wall Street banker, why are you paying him?" I asked as I just remembered what she'd said earlier.

"Because he's the devil." She laughed and stood up. "Okay, I should get going. Thanks once again, Lila. I'll see you in a month." And with that she hurried out of my apartment so she could hurry to the airport and hopefully not miss her flight.

"Bye, Danielle," I called after her as I sat back and continued to sip on my wine. I tried to imagine what her brother looked like, but then laughed at myself. I was horribly busy with work right now and it seemed as if he was really busy as well, so I'm sure it's unlikely that we would see each other at all asides from when he picked up the keys. I grabbed the remote control and turned the TV on to try to find a cooking show before I got up to take Frosty on his evening walk.

"*O*h come on," I said tapping my foot against the wooden floor as I waited for my doorbell to ring. "Where are you, Carter?" I muttered under my breath as I stared at my watch. Five more minutes had passed, and he still wasn't here. I was going to miss the next train which meant I was going to miss my connecting train, which meant I was going to be late for work. I walked back to the living room from the hallway and sat on the couch, trying not to look at my watch again. I grabbed my phone and scrolled to my text messages. He'd said he would be here at 8:30 a.m. to get the keys. Had I somehow read it wrong? Did he mean 8:30 p.m.? It was now 9:00 a.m. How could he say 8:30 a.m. and be this late? He had to know I had to work. I typed into the phone and sent him another text message.

"*Hey, Carter, it's me, Lila, just checking you're still coming this morning? :)*" I added a smiley face, so he wouldn't know how annoyed I was, just in case my text message read as passive aggressive.

"*Yup.*" He text back. I waited to see if he was going to say more than that. Like a *sorry, I'm late*, or *the trains are delayed* or something. But nope, all he said was "yup" like he wasn't already thirty minutes behind.

"*Do you have an ETA?*" I typed finally as I realized another five minutes had passed and still nothing. I watched the screen intensely as I saw the three dots appear to show me that he was typing a response, but then they stopped. They stopped and no message came. "Are you frigging joking me?" I hissed at the screen. How could he start typing a response and then just not respond, knowing he was already late. Why wouldn't he just tell me he was running late? He had absolutely no respect for my time. No respect at all. I knew he was busy as well, but come on now. He was the one that had texted me to say that this morning would be best for him to get the keys as had some gig tonight and didn't know when he'd be around. I wondered to myself if he was really going to be able to take care of Frosty properly, but he knew what he was doing. It was his sister's dog after all, he would have to make the time. I gnawed on my lower lip as I realized another ten minutes had passed and still not a word from Carter. He was starting to really piss me off now. Did he have no respect for my time at all?

"*Hey are you going to be here soon?*" I sent another text message. And I didn't add a smiley face this time. I didn't care that he hadn't responded as yet. No one could call me psycho for constantly texting in a situation like this.

"Yup," he responded immediately, and I screamed. Yup? What the hell did yup mean? I was normally an even-keeled person, but this morning was already off to a rough start. Frosty had gone potty on Danielle's rug so I'd had to clean that up before I took him on his walk and then he had been so busy trying to chase every squirrel that he saw that he didn't want to go potty for ages. I'd had to take a five-minute shower, had nicked myself while shaving and then to make matters worse, my favorite black blazer had felt too tight when I'd put it on, so I'd had to wear my gray suit instead. And I hated my gray suit.

"*How long will you be? I have to get to work and now I'm already running late.*" I typed out again. Let him feel bad for being tardy. I didn't care if he was some hot shot banker and musician, he needed to respect other people's time.

Ding Dong. The doorbell rang as soon as I pressed send, but I didn't feel guilty. "Finally," I mumbled as I jumped up off of the couch and hurried to the front door and pulled it open hastily. "You made it," I muttered before even making eye contact with him.

"Hi there, Lila, right? I'm Carter. Sorry for the delay. The line in the coffee shop was way too long, and I wanted to get you a latte and bagel with lox and cream cheese. Danielle told me they were your favorites." The man in front of me gave me an easy, lazy smile, his blue eyes were open and friendly and his perfect white teeth gleamed at me.

"Hi." That was all I managed to squeak out as I stared at Carter. Danielle had understated just how good-looking her brother was. He wasn't just good-looking. He was gorgeous. Absolutely gorgeous. He stood at about six-four with a solid muscular build. He had dark golden blond hair that surrounded his face perfectly. His blue eyes were azure in color and reminded me of the ocean colors I'd seen in the Caribbean.

"Here you go," he said, and he handed me a small cup from my favorite coffee shop and a brown bag with a still warm bagel inside. "I hope that they are as good as you remember them being."

"Thanks," I said as I took the cup and bag from him. I gave him a huge smile, all my anger having faded away as soon as I'd seen his smile. "Would you like to come inside?"

"Willing to share some of that bagel?" He grinned and gave me a small wink as he walked into my apartment. He made my hallway feel like it was a part of a doll's house and my heart raced as I stood next to him and stared at his muscles up close and personal. "I forgot to get one for myself."

"Oh, of course." I grinned at him. "Come on in," I said and waved him to follow me down the hallway to the kitchen.

"Should I take my shoes off?" he asked as he paused next to the door. He was wearing a white T-shirt that said,

No Sleep Till Brooklyn, and blue faded jeans that clung to his hips.

"No, that's okay." I swallowed hard to stop myself from telling him that he could take his T-shirt off if he wanted. I didn't know what had come over me. I couldn't stop looking at his biceps and imagine his big hands all over me. I reddened as I realized that I was totally fantasizing over him and I'd just met him.

"Okay, are you sure you have time for the bagel?" He gave me a boyish grin as I took two plates out of the cupboard. "You said you were running late in your text, right?"

"I'm already late." I wrinkled my nose at him as I grabbed a knife to cut the bagel in half. "What's thirty more minutes going to do?"

"You'll have to let me get you an Uber into your job," he said as he took the plate from me and grabbed the bagel. "Mmm," He made a noise as he took a bite and chewed. "This is delicious."

"Glad you approve," I said and took a bite myself. The bagel was toasted perfectly and had just the right amount of cream cheese and lox. "Yummy," I said as I swallowed. I placed the plate on the table and then opened the fridge door. "Would you like some orange juice?"

"Yes, please," he said, and he walked over to the fridge and stood next to me. "Thanks for your hospitality by the way." He ran his hand through his hair and smiled at me. "Danielle told me you were nice and I guess she was right."

"She's great." I smiled back at him, ignoring the urge to pat my hair to make sure that it was in place. "I'm so glad that she's my neighbor."

"You just moved in recently, right?" he said as he took the glass of orange juice. His blue eyes gazed into mine as if he were genuinely interested in the answer.

"Yes." I nodded. "I just moved to New York about two years ago. I started working at this firm about six months ago and moved in here three months ago."

"You're a lawyer, right?"

"Yes. I went to law school at the University of Iowa."

"Go Hawkeyes," he said, and I looked at him in surprise. "I might not look like it, but I'm a huge fan of college football."

"Oh?"

"Yeah, my family is from Ohio so we're Ohio State fans, but I can respect the Iowa team, though they're not as good as the Buckeyes."

"You wish." I laughed. Carter Stevens was the last person I would have assumed to have been into college football. He just looked too cool and sexy to be into something so every day.

"So you came here after law school? And started working for the firm?"

"I moved here and worked for a non-profit, but then upgraded to a firm." I made a face. "More money and all that jazz."

"I see." He nodded. "And you're single?"

"Maybe," I said coyly, surprised by his question. "Why do you ask?" I bit down on my lower lip and gazed at him as he finished eating his bagel.

"Because I'd be devastated to find out you had a boyfriend."

"Danielle was right." I laughed. "You really are a huge flirt, aren't you?"

"I'm not a flirt." He shook his head. "Well, not with everyone."

"I'm one of the lucky ones, am I?"

"Of course, you're a very lucky one." He winked at me and then before I could blink he was reaching over and lightly removing a random piece of bagel from the side of my mouth. I watched as he popped it inside of his. "Didn't want to waste any of it now."

"You." I was speechless. Had he really just eaten a crumb from the side of my mouth?

"Yes, what about me?"

"I, I just don't know what to say." I shook my head at him. It was weird to know that we'd just met. A part of me felt so comfortable with him; as if I'd known him for years.

"You have beautiful brown eyes," he stated then and within seconds he was singing "Brown Eyed Girl" by Van Morrison; one of my absolute favorite songs. "Do you remember when we used to sing . . ." His voice was deep and smooth and I joined him in the chorus, even though my voice sounded like something from the reject episodes of *American Idol*. My voice trailed off as he continued singing as I didn't know all the words and I just stood there sipping my coffee watching this absolutely gorgeous man sing to me. It was surreal, it was ridiculous, and I absolutely loved it. Things like this just didn't happen to me. And while a part of me was extremely ill-at-ease and slightly embarrassed, there was just something about Carter that made his being so over-the-top seem quite normal.

"So, brown-eyed girl, what are you doing tonight?"

"Tonight?" I stared at him wondering where he was going with this conversation. Could he also be into me?

"Yeah tonight." He grinned. "I have a gig at Rockwood Music Hall, maybe you'd like to come?"

"Um, well, I work," I stammered.

"You're telling me you have to work all night?"

"No, I'm just saying that I'm already late for work and I have a lot of files to go through today. We're going to trial next week, and well, I just don't know when I'll be free."

"Make yourself free." He gave me an impish grin. "I'll make it worth your while."

"Oh yeah?" I asked, loving the way he was so easy and teasing with me. "You don't even know me."

"Well, I know where you live." His phone beeped then, and he grabbed it from his pocket. I watched as he made a face. "But that's my cue to go and check on Frosty. I need to change and head off to work myself."

"Aw, okay," I said, feeling disappointed, but knowing it was for the best. I could talk to Carter Stevens all day and night. "I was wondering what investment firm you worked for that you could wear jeans and a T-shirt."

"Hey, that's how we do it on Wall Street these days." He laughed and then his face grew slightly serious. "But I really should be going now. Thanks for the keys. And for looking after Frosty for a couple of days. I hope you can make it tonight, the show is at eight. If not, I guess I'll see you around this place."

"Yeah, I guess so," I said, suddenly feeling sad. What if I never really saw him? I mean, I didn't see Danielle all that often. He was hot and sexy and he was flirting with me and I liked it. Granted he most probably wasn't going to be the love of my life, but he could be the fun of my life. I needed some fun. He seemed like the perfect guy to have some fun with. I was going to go to that show tonight even if it meant I had to go back to the office afterward. I knew it would be worth it.

"Girls Just Want to Have Fun"

"I'll make it worth your while. I'll make it worth your while?" I groaned as I shook my head at Frosty. "What the hell was I thinking?" Frosty just sat there staring at me with his big brown dopey eyes. "She most probably thinks I'm an idiot." I pulled my jeans off and threw them onto the ground. I knew Danielle would not be happy that I was already leaving my clothes all over the place, but what she didn't know wouldn't kill her. "Where the hell is my suit?" I rifled through the suitcase I'd brought with me and pulled out a blue shirt and some clean boxers. I couldn't seem to find any of my suits though. "Fuck it," I growled under my breath. I must have left my suits on the bed in my rush. I'd woken up late and had to rush up here to grab the keys from Lila. I had been very pleasantly surprised when she'd opened the door.

Danielle hadn't told me how hot her new neighbor was with her doe-like brown eyes, blond hair and very shapely body. It didn't hurt that she seemed to have a fun personality that matched her looks. I'd been pleasantly surprised when she'd sang along to "Brown Eyed Girl" with me. Granted, she couldn't sing for shit, but at least she'd tried. I wasn't used to women that weren't afraid to make a fool of themselves.

"Do you think she's going to come tonight?" I continued to talk to Frosty as if he actually understood what I was talking about. This was why I didn't have my own dog. People with dogs became crazy. "She's not going to come. I bet she's still annoyed I was late. Do you think she was annoyed?" I rolled my eyes as Frosty started sniffing his butt. "She's a lawyer," I said as I debated what to do. I couldn't go into work like this. And I didn't want to go all the way back to the Upper West Side now. I'd just call in and get ready for the show tonight. Plus I needed to go through my finances to make sure that I had calculated everything correctly before I gave in my resignation at the end of the month.

I was finally ready to pursue my dreams of becoming a full-time musician and getting out of the rat race. Not that I'd told anyone in my family though. I wasn't sure they'd approve; especially Danielle. Even though I was the older brother she always acted like she was the boss of me. I loved her, but everything I did she seemed to disapprove of. Well, maybe that was due to the fact that I'd dated several of her friends and broken their hearts. Not that that had been my fault though. I'd barely gone out with any of them before they started acting all attached and clingy. I paused as I thought about Lila. Maybe it wasn't such a good idea for her to come tonight. I didn't want her to fall for me or anything like that. No matter how hot I thought she was. I didn't need to complicate this living situation. Danielle was going to be gone for a month at the minimum she'd said and I couldn't have dogs in my apartment, so if something went bad with Lila, I'd have to stay here still. And I didn't want things to be awkward. Though if the sex was good enough I could deal with awkward for a few weeks. I could deal with a lot for good sex.

My phone started ringing then, and I grabbed my jeans up from the floor to pull my phone out of the pocket. "'Sup, man?" I said as I answered the phone.

"Whatcha doing?" Harley growled into the phone. He always sounded as if he were angry, but that was just his voice. It was deep and husky, just like him.

"Well, I was supposed to be at work, but I'm taking the day off," I said. "And no I can't meet you for breakfast. I'm up here in Brooklyn."

"Brooklyn?" For a husky country guy, Harley was a bit of a snob. He never liked to leave Manhattan unless it was for a gig.

"I told you I'm looking after my sister's dog," I said, and I looked over to see what Frosty was doing. He was now sniffing at my pants and I grabbed them up. I didn't need the mutt chewing up my favorite pair of jeans.

"Oh yeah, so you're going to be leaving from there for Rockwood tonight?" Harley was the drummer in our band and I knew he was hoping to pregame before the show.

"Yeah, man. I'm staying out here for a month or so."

"What are you doing with your place then?" he asked, his voice curious and hopeful.

"I'm not letting you crash in any of the rooms, dude," I said in a firm voice. The last time I'd let him stay over and look after my pad he'd had a threesome with two middle-aged women from Texas that hadn't wanted to leave; even when I'd showed up and told them he didn't live there.

"Aw, c'mon, Carter."

"Why did you call me, Harley?" I changed the subject and walked through to the kitchen to see if Danielle had any coffee. I needed some caffeine.

"Fine. So my cousin Jimbo called me and he said that he heard that a record exec was going to be there tonight."

"Oh yeah?" I perked up. "From what label?"

"Universal maybe?" he said and I could tell that he couldn't really remember. There were only three things that Harley cared about: the drums, women, and beer. "But yeah, that'll be cool, right?"

"Yeah, that'll be cool." I rifled through the cupboards to see if there was anything close to coffee beans or even instant available to drink. "Hey, dude, I'll see you tonight, okay? I gotta go."

"Right now. Rock 'n roll, baby," he said and hung up. I laughed as I placed the phone down on the counter. I looked at my watch and wondered if Lila had left home as of yet? Maybe she had some coffee she could lend me. I ran through the kitchen to the front door and knocked on Lila's door with my fingers crossed.

"Hey," she said, opening the door. There was a surprised look on her face as she gazed at me and as her eyes went lower I could see her blushing. Oh shit! I'd forgotten that I'd taken my jeans off and was standing here in just my T-shirt and boxer briefs.

"Hey, I don't suppose you have any coffee do you?" I asked naturally, pretending that it was completely normal for me to be standing here in my tight white briefs that didn't hide much of anything. Not that I cared. I had nothing to be ashamed of down below. Nothing at all.

"Coffee?" She blinked at me and I could tell that she was confused. "I thought you were rushing to work?" Her beautiful brown eyes stared into mine and I watched as she tucked some runaway blond hairs behind her ears. Her lips puckered in a confused way. They were plump and pink and looked like they were just waiting to be kissed.

"Yeah, I was, but I left my suit at home, so I'm just going to chill today."

"Oh, wow," she said and I could see her staring at me wonderingly. She most probably thought I was some sort of sexy arrogant asshole. "Um, let me check if I have any coffee beans." She walked away from the door and I stayed in the hallway. I could see Frosty standing at my front door peering out curiously. "Here we go," she said, and she walked back to me with a small bag of beans. "These are beans from Kenya, dark roast. Enjoy."

"Oh you sure I can have these?" I asked, knowing African beans were pretty pricey.

"Yeah, you can pay me back in another way," she said with an impish smile and I watched as her two front teeth bit down on her lower lip. I wondered if she was deliberately trying to tempt me. She had to know the effect she had on me, didn't she?

"Well that sounds like a deal I can definitely make." I gave her my half-smile that drove all the women crazy and she just laughed girlishly at me and pushed the bag into my hand.

"I'm sorry to be rude, but I'm about to leave now and have to go." She grabbed her handbag from the table and I watched as she slipped her feet into a pair of black pumps. She closed the door behind her and stood next to me. She gazed up at me expectantly and I wondered if she was hoping for a kiss. Maybe we were on the same page after all. "Uh, excuse me." She grinned at me. "Can I pass?"

"Oh yeah, sorry." I moved to the side. I was blocking her entrance way, and she needed to get past me; she wasn't just standing there waiting for a kiss.

"No worries," she said with a small smile. "It was nice meeting you today, Carter. Hopefully I can make it tonight."

"I'll have my fingers crossed." I said honestly. "And it was great meeting you as well, Lila. I think this is going to be the beginning of a beautiful friendship."

$\approx$

*T*he music was loud as I walked into Rockwood. I recognized the band on the stage; they were a young jazz group, and I knew they weren't getting paid for being there tonight. I watched as one of their girlfriends walked around with a hat collecting tips from the patrons. None of them put their hands in their pockets. They weren't there to listen to them. They were here to listen to me. I watched as a huddle of women in the corner looked over at me whispering. I gave them a huge smile, but didn't go over to them. Instead I headed to the bar. I needed a drink.

"Hey, Carter, you're here early." Betsy, the cute red headed bartender handed me a beer. "Here you go."

"Thanks." I grinned as I grabbed the glass. "Figured I would see who else was playing here tonight."

"Some jazz kids. I think they go to Julliard." She nodded toward the enthusiastic youngsters on the stage. "They're good, though this crowd doesn't really appreciate their brand of good."

"You know jazz doesn't sell as well as rock and roll." I laughed and looked around the room. I saw many familiar faces as I surveyed the room. We'd really developed a small cult following in our two years of playing. It made me feel proud to have brought a real crowd out tonight. Lila would be impressed if she came. I hoped she was going to come.

"Shannon was asking about you." Betsy leaned forward with a wicked smile. "She'll be happy to see you."

"She's working tonight?" I asked and tried not to groan. Shannon was the other bartender. A hottie from Atlanta that had moved up to New York a year ago. We'd gone on a couple of dates a couple of months ago, but she'd been looking for something much more serious than I was looking to give. We hadn't even hooked up, which I was glad about because she'd been blowing up my phone weekly asking if I wanted to go out. I'd politely declined at first, but I'd ignored her last couple of texts.

"Yup." Betsy grinned. I knew she was itching to see some drama go down. Betsy and I had never had anything, but she'd hooked up with Harley in the past and while she liked me, she was eager to see me and the guys get into woman trouble. It seemed to make her feel better about life. She was a cute girl, and I'd not really understood what she'd seen in Harley in the first place, but I guess women just have this thing for musicians, hot or not.

"Oh well, that's cool," I said nonchalantly, hoping that Shannon wouldn't pull anything if Lila showed up. That would be all I needed. I wasn't really sure why I cared so much. It wasn't as if I even knew Lila. We'd barely even met. But there was just something about her cute face and her passive aggressive texts that had gotten to me. I wanted to see if she would be as exciting in the bedroom as I imagined her to be. Not that I just wanted to get to know her just for sex; I also enjoyed talking to her. She seemed fun. I wanted to roll my eyes at myself. She seemed fun? Really Carter.

"Here she is." Betsy's excited voice interrupted my reverie as Shannon came to stand next to her. "Hey, Shannon, look who it is," she said as if Shannon couldn't and wouldn't recognize me standing here right in front of her. I put on my most dazzling smile and gazed into Shannon's almost black irises.

"Hi there, how you doing?" I said as if I hadn't been ignoring her.

"Forget it, Carter." There was no smile on her face as she responded to me, her ebony skin glowing. "I don't have time for your BS."

"My BS?" I threw my hands up. "I'm offended."

"Yeah right." Shannon gave me a look and then gave Betsy a look as if to say, are you buying this crap? "Betsy, I'm knocking off early, okay? Stallone wants to take me for drinks."

"Yeah, no worries." Betsy shrugged. "More tips for me."

"Um, is anyone else working? This place is packed tonight." I looked around the room and even more people had piled in while we'd been talking.

"I guess they'll have to line up then, won't they?" Shannon gave me a look, her beautiful model face looking satisfied. Aw, this was part of her plan to get me back. I got it now. "Bye," she said, and I watched as she sashayed from behind the bar and left the room.

"You do realize you're going to be slammed, right?" I looked at Betsy who was grinning.

"Dude, that's double tips for me." She shrugged and then winked at me. "That went better than expected, eh?"

"Disappointed?"

"Slightly." She laughed and then she shooed me away. "Move now, boy, there are other people lining up to be served."

"Bye, Betsy," I said as I stepped away from the bar and looked toward the entrance to see if Lila had somehow arrived in the last couple of minutes. I pulled out my phone to see if she'd texted me for directions or anything, but I suppose Google Maps could have given her any information she needed. "Are you going to come, Lila Delilah?" I mumbled as I stared at the screen that had a few missed calls, but no missed texts from Lila. I didn't know why I cared so much. I never cared this much. And then because sometimes good things do come to those that wait, I felt something in my body stiffening as I heard a familiar laugh. I looked back toward the entrance and there she stood, in a short black dress with a low cut V-neck. She looked amazing and I couldn't keep my eyes off of her as she laughed again at something the bouncer was saying to her. Finally, she walked into the club and I walked over to greet her.

"Hey, sexy," I said as soon as my eyes met hers. She grinned at me and I gave her a lazy smile as I admired her body, so curvaceous and soft. Her long blond hair was hanging straight past her shoulders and it looked silky, like fine spun gold thread.

"Hey," she replied, her voice almost a whisper, as if she were shy. Her eyes bore into mine seductively and I could feel the sexual tension between us rising. It was easy to forget that we'd only met that morning.

"I like that necklace," I said and reached over to touch the fine piece of silver that was hanging between the curves of her breasts. My fingers grazed down her neck as they played with the chain and I stopped just short of her heaving bosoms. I could see the vein in her neck throbbing as we stood there close to each other.

"Oops, sorry." She gasped, a small smile on her face as she fell into me. Some guy having pushed past us to get to the bar.

"Nothing to be sorry about." My hands clung to her waist. Her body felt warm and I could feel her heart beating against me. I wanted to lean down and kiss her, but instead I thanked her for coming out.

"No worries, thanks for inviting me. This is awesome and I can't wait to see you perform. You play guitar, right?" she asked reminding me why she was here. I wondered what she would say if I told her all I wanted to do was take her in the back room, lift up her skirt and bend her over.

"And I sing," I said as I nodded; not daring to tell her how badly I wanted her. "We're a local band, but we have a lot of support."

"This is a cool spot. I've never been to Rockwood Music Hall before," she said and looked around the venue. My eyes were glued to her neck, and how delicate and feminine it was. I was also enjoying the smell of her. She smelled like fresh strawberries. I wondered if that was her natural odor or her bodywash. She'd obviously gone home to change. She certainly hadn't been wearing that sexy dress this morning when she was headed to work.

"We're going to go on in about ten minutes," I whispered into her ear wanting to tease her before I went on stage. I allowed my tongue to lightly touch her inner ear to see how she was going to respond. Was she feeling the heat between us as badly as I was? I smiled as I got my answer. Not only did she not pull away but I could also feel her body trembling. She was definitely feeling it and before I knew what was happening, I could feel her fingers on mine touching me softly. I could feel myself hardening next to her and I knew that if this continued at the pace we were currently going, I'd be lifting up her dress and doing naughty things to her right here in front of everyone. "I have to go to the back and grab my gear and get ready," I said hastily. There was going to be a music exec here tonight. I still had to go on and play, no matter how badly I just wanted to be with Lila. "However, let's get a drink when I'm done, yeah?" I stared into her eyes and all I could think about was feeling her softly parted lips on my now very hard cock.

"Just a drink?" she asked, with a teasing smile and I almost groaned out loud.

"It's never just a drink," I said with a wink and then I leaned forward and kissed her, my hands bringing her body in even closer to mine so that she could feel my hardness against her. I knew it was a bold move, but I was feeling in a bold mood. "Tonight we're going to make some sweet music, baby," I said and slipped my tongue into her mouth so that I could taste her sweetness on my lips before I went onto the stage to perform.

"Okay," she whispered as she kissed me back passionately, her fingers on the back of my shoulders. I broke away from her and gave her one last wink before I walked toward the hallway that would take me to the back room where my guitar was waiting for me.

"Hey, man, who's that hottie?" Harley slapped me on the shoulder as I walked into the back room.

"What?"

"That hot blonde." He smacked his lips together. "With the big rack."

"Really, Harley?" I frowned at the way he was talking about Lila.

"What?" He twirled his drumsticks between his fingers and began nodding his head up and down to some beat in his mind. "Does she or does she not have a big rack?" He winked at me. "I sure noticed you admiring it."

"Harley, just concentrate on tonight. Did you see the execs?" I walked over to the corner of the room and picked up my guitar and searched through my case for my cables so I could attach it to the amp on stage. "You got the setlist?"

"Yeah." He nodded. "Bruno wanted to know if we could include some Hendrix tonight."

"No, man, we need to stick to the setlist." I shook my head and looked around the room to see if the bass player was in the room with us. "Where is Bruno? We're going on in ten minutes."

"He went to the restroom." Harley shredded an air guitar. "He'll be back. He said that Lucas will be able to join us tonight on keys."

"Sweet." I started to tune my guitar. "That'll be good. He's nearly here."

"Yeah, man, yeah." Harley nodded. "So you going to introduce me to the hottie?"

"Why don't you just worry about Betsy." I raised an eyebrow at him and he groaned.

"Low blow, man, low blow."

"When you go low, I go even lower." I laughed and started ripping some chords. "And her name is Lila by the way."

"Lyla?" He grinned. "Like the Oasis song?"

"No, it's L I L A."

"You know how to spell her name already?"

"Danielle sent me her name with her number."

"Oh, she's Danielle's friend?" He made a face. He knew better than to mess with Danielle or any of her friends. He'd tried to hit on Danielle a long time ago and it hadn't ended well for him.

"Yup, they live next door to each other," I said before I couldn't stop myself.

"Oh shit, it's going to go down." Harley started dancing around. "Bow chicka bow wow."

"Really, dude?" I shook my head and looked at my

watch. "We need to head out. We're on in a few minutes. You better text Bruno and Lucas and tell them to hurry the fuck up."

"Yes, bossman."

"You ready?"

"Let's rock 'n roll, dude." Harley high-fived me and we grinned at each other, the excitement palpable in the air. I loved performing. It made me feel so alive, like I was on top of the world and flying through the sky with a crowd of people on the ground just watching me as I soared back and forth. The crowds cheering for me made my heart beat just that little bit faster, seeing the smiles on people's faces as they danced and sang along to the music always thrilled me. It was in those moments that I actually felt like I connected with humankind. Most days, I thought that most humans were shit, but when it came to music and performing it was all about love. The love of music brought us together, and it was the most epic shit ever.

~

"Any special requests?" I called out to the crowd. "We have two songs left before we have to get off the stage." I listened to the boos and grinned out at the crowd. I could see the two music execs standing by the bar at the back, standing out like sore thumbs in their suits. They seemed to be impressed by the crowds and that made me happy, but not as happy as I felt as I watched Lila dancing back and forth to the music, her body in perfect timing to the beat of each song. Her long hair swayed back and forth as she moved and she looked like she was having a good time. I made eye contact with her a few times and she'd blushed and lowered her head slightly as I'd sang directly to her. I liked that she was a little shy at times. She was an enigma to me. Sometimes she was really bold and outgoing, like some sort of vixen and other times she was shy and innocent. I couldn't read her, but then I didn't know her that well yet. I intended to get to know her really well, real soon. "What about you, Lila?" I pointed to her in the crowd and ushered her to come forward in the crowd. "Any special request?"

"What about 'Girls Just Want to Have Fun'?" she said, her voice loud as she shouted and did a little shimmy.

"Girls just want to have fun, huh?" I watched her body moving as she sang the song out loud for me. The crowd was loud and packed, but in that moment, it felt like we were the only two people there. "Do you just want to have fun?" I called out again and a bunch of guys next to the stage hollered and high-fived each other. I watched as one tall guy in a Steelers shirt walked over to Lila and started talking to her. I frowned as I watched her smiling back at him. Was she flirting with this guy while we were having a moment?

"Yo, Carter. What's next?" Harley hollered at me from the back of the stage.

"Let's do some Kiss," I said, looking away from Lila and the Steelers jerk. "'Rock and Roll All Nite,' all right boys?" I looked behind me and they all nodded. Bruno played a couple of chords and I counted down as I took a couple of steps back. "A one, a one, two, three, four," I said and then began to sing my heart out. Though for some reason I wasn't as caught up in the song as I normally was. My eyes couldn't stop watching Lila with her new beau. She was now laughing at something he was saying as if he was the funniest person on the earth. What the hell was her problem? Was she one of those people that came out to shows to pick up guys instead of listen to music. I conveniently forgot that she'd come out to this show for me and that I was hoping that we would hook up tonight.

~

*T*he crowd went crazy when we ended the last song and they began chanting the band name.

"Thanks, guys. That was Harley Driver on the drums, Bruno Smith on the bass, Lucas Hamilton on the keys and I'm Carter Stevens on guitar and vocals. We're The Bedroom Rockers, thanks for coming out tonight and hope to see you soon. You can find us by the bar if you want to buy us a drink." I put the microphone back in the holder and took a final bow before exiting the stage.

"Hey, man, you rock." One of the guys that was in the group with Steelers guy approached me as soon as I walked off of the stage. "Can I get you a beer?"

"Sure." I nodded and gave him a quick smile as I looked around the room to locate Lila. She was staring at me with a wide smile on her face and clapping her hands. I grinned at her and was about to blow her a kiss when I noticed Steelers guy was still standing there and he had his hand on her waist.

"Enjoy the show?" I walked over to Lila with a tight smile. Maybe she wasn't feeling the same chemistry I was or maybe any man would do.

"It was absolutely amazing." She nodded and then looked up to the guy next to her. "Didn't you think so, Dan?" Dan? Did she know this fool?

"Dude, you were great." He stuck his hand out to shake mine. "Me and my friends have been following you guys from the beginning. We drove in from Philly for the show tonight."

"Cool, cool." I shook his hand, his grip was weak.

Loser. "Do you guys know each other?" I addressed Lila. All of a sudden I wasn't so pleased that she was wearing such a revealing dress, but I knew that was hypocritical of me. I'd enjoyed ogling the tops of her breasts when I'd thought the display was for me. Now I wasn't so happy that every Tom, Dick, and Harry in the bar was getting a glimpse of the goods.

"No, we just met tonight," Lila said with a small smile, but her face looked unsure, as if she could sense I was pissed. "Everything okay?" She looked concerned.

"It's fine." I nodded. "There were some music execs here tonight. I was just thinking of the set wondering if we impressed them."

"You guys were great." She leaned forward and touched my arm. "Really great."

"Glad you think so," I said abruptly as I saw that Dan's hand was now on her lower back. "Come with me," I said and grabbed her hand and pulled her toward me. "Nice meeting you, Dan, but Lila and I need to chat," I said as he stood there looking slightly dumbfounded.

"What are you doing?" She looked up at me in surprise.

"Who was that guy?" I blinked down at her, trying not to stare at her parted lips. "You know he wanted to fuck you, right?"

"What?" Her jaw dropped, and she blushed. "You don't know that."

"I saw how he was looking at you. He wanted to take you outside, bend you over and fuck you," I said crudely.

"Wow, okay," she said, her face now looking annoyed with me. "Good to know."

"Hey." I stopped suddenly, knowing I was overreacting. "Sorry, I was just being protective of you. You're my sister's friend and I don't want to see you getting screwed over by some jerk."

"You don't even know him." She stood in front of me, her face peering up at me. I could see she was processing something in her mind and I was worried she was going to think I was too much and leave.

"Let me get you that drink I promised you," I said quickly before she could tell me she was tired and had to leave.

"I don't know." She chewed on her lower lip. "It's been a long day and I should be getting home."

"Hey," I said, and I pulled her toward me. "Sorry for being so crazy just now. I'm a little stressed. I'm about to quit my job and become a full-time musician and so I was really worried about how tonight was going to go. I really wanted to impress the execs, you know?" What I said was mostly true, I did want to impress the music executives, but that wasn't why I'd acted like a jerk. For some reason I'd been really annoyed at the way Dan had been looking at and touching Lila.

"Aw, I see." She nodded, her face thoughtful. "So you're leaving Wall Street?"

"Yeah." I paused as I felt her hand on my arm. "I figure now's the time. I'm single, no kids, no responsibilities, no debts."

"Yeah that's true." She smiled. "Low overhead, I guess."

"As low as it can be for New York." I laughed. "It helps that I don't have a girlfriend and don't want one. No need for expensive dinners and gifts." I saw her face freeze, and I wondered if my honesty had turned her off. I hoped not. I didn't want her to walk away from me, but I didn't want to lie to her. I didn't know what this chemistry between us was but I didn't want a relationship. I needed to concentrate on my career as a musician. I was already behind the game when it came to the industry. I was thirty and music was a young man's game. I didn't have spare time or energy for the drama or time commitment it took to be in a serious relationship.

"I see," she said and then she just laughed, and the sound shocked and surprised me. That wasn't the response I'd been expecting. That wasn't the response I'd gotten from any of the other ladies I'd had this conversation with before. Granted, I hadn't really cared when they'd gotten upset.

"What's so funny?" I frowned as she continued laughing, throwing her head back and shaking her head.

"You," she said as she finally stopped laughing and wiped her eyes. "Don't worry about me wanting you to take me out for fancy dinners or me having any expectations of you buying me any gifts. I don't want a relationship with you, Carter."

"You don't?" My eyes narrowed. Was she trying to say she wasn't interested in me? There was no way she had been faking it.

"No, I don't. Frankly, I think you'd make an awful boyfriend," she said earnestly.

"Oh?" My jaw hardened. She thought I would make a bad boyfriend?

"I don't even know you and you've already shown your bossy and jealous side." She rolled her eyes. "I couldn't even imagine what you would be like to date."

"I'm not bossy or jealous." I denied her accusations. What the hell was she talking about?

"Look, let's not argue." She leaned in and gave me a quick kiss on the lips. "You're not looking for a relationship and neither am I. Let's grab a drink and then head back to my place."

"Oh yeah?" I held the back of her head and kissed her back passionately. "You want to go back to your place?"

"Yeah, we can have some fun."

"Some fun?" I kissed the side of her neck.

"Yes, some fun. Girls just want to have fun, remember?" She leaned forward and trailed the tip of her tongue along my upper lip and I felt my body stiffening. "Go and get me my drink and hurry up," she said as she pulled back. There was a devious look in her chestnut brown eyes and I growled under my breath. This woman was trouble with a capital T and I loved it.

"I'll be right back," I said as I hurried to the bar. I could see Harley standing next to the music execs and calling me over, but I ignored him. I couldn't think about anything right now asides from getting Lila her drink and then going back to her place. I was excited to see just how much fun she wanted to have.

"Betsy, give me two of your best cocktails, stat," I said as I called her over to me. One of the best things about being a musician meant I never had to wait at the bar for a drink and the other patrons didn't get mad because they knew you were with the band and expected you to get treated like an A-lister. Even though I wasn't an A-Lister in anyone's eyes, it felt nice to have some perks.

"Sweet or strong?" Betsy said as she walked over to me, leaving the guy she was serving mid-pour. I grinned at her; Betsy was my girl.

"Both."

"Who's the girl?" she asked me curiously as she grabbed two glasses and a bottle of vodka.

"My date for the night."

"Your date?" Her jaw dropped, and I laughed. "I've never heard you refer to them as your date before."

"I'm not a philistine, Betsy." I rolled my eyes at her.

"It's not like we're getting married. She's just a girl I met that wants to have some fun."

"Of course." Betsy just shook her head. "God forbid they want something more."

"Women know what they're getting with me." I reached over and rubbed her hand. "You should be happy that I'm one of the honest guys out there."

"Yeah, I'm so happy," she said as she shook a stainless steel mixer and got ready to pour it.

"Have a great evening, Betsy." I pulled a twenty-dollar bill and left it on the bar for her as a tip. The drinks were free for the musicians, but I always made sure to tip the bartenders well. It made them happy and ensured we had a continuing good relationship.

"Thanks, Carter." She beamed and tucked the twenty into her bra. "I hope you have a great night." She winked at me as she handed me the two drinks and I just took them and nodded. She was not the only one that was hoping I had a great night. I was hoping it was going to be a lot more than just great.

LILA

"**S**hape of You"

"**Y**ou want to get out of here?" Carter whispered into my ear, his breath warm against my skin.

"Yes." I nodded as I quickly downed the rest of the delicious cocktail he had bought me. I could see Dan and his friends staring at us from a couple of feet away and I just smiled at him. I'd been surprised when Dan had come up to me during Carter's set. He'd been a good-looking jock looking type and if I wasn't here with Carter, I would definitely have spent a couple of minutes trying to get to know him better. However, I had eyes for no one but Carter right now. Even though he was fast proving to be a bit of a jerk. Well, not a jerk exactly, but a bit overbearing. I was finding it hard to read him. He seemed so sweet, but also a little bit egotistical. I couldn't believe that he'd found it necessary to tell me he didn't want anything. Like he thought I wanted him so badly.

He'd been shocked when I'd started laughing. I hadn't been able to believe how arrogant he was, like he thought he was God's gift to women. Granted he was sexy as fuck and he had a raspy beautiful voice that had given me chills when he'd performed tonight. Not that I was going to tell him that. His head was big enough as it was.

"My place or yours?"

"Do you mean Danielle's place or yours?" I smiled at him teasingly. "And definitely mine, I would feel weird hooking up in your sisters bed."

"Who says it has to be in the bed?" He winked.

"The first time has to be in the bed." I winked back at him and he growled before he leaned in to kiss me. His lips were firm against mine and his fingers pressed into the back of my waist as he kissed me hard and passionately. I felt his hands running up my back and to my hair as his fingers ran through my locks.

"I want you, Lila," he growled as he pulled me into him so that my body was pressed into his. I melted against him and kissed him back. I'd never felt this immediate and complete sexual attraction to anyone before in my life. I'd always wondered what it would be like to just submit to my physical wants and tonight I was just going to do it. I hadn't lied to Carter when I'd said I just want to have fun. I did. I mean, yeah I ultimately wanted a relationship, but I wasn't going to stop myself from just living my life. So what if he didn't want a relationship? I didn't even know if he would make a good boyfriend. Just because I was attracted to him didn't mean that he had potential to be the love of my life. I'd dated too many losers in the past and I was not going to succumb to the idea that lust meant love anymore. Carter Stevens was hot. There was no denying that. Carter Stevens turned me on. There was no denying that. I wanted Carter Stevens to show me all the things he could do to me that would make me a true believer, and I didn't care what else came of it. I was allowed to have some fun and enjoy some good sex. And I wasn't going to feel badly about it.

"I want you too." I put my hands on the crook of his neck and ran my fingers through his hair. I breathed him in deeply, he smelled like a combination of sweat and after-shave and it was thoroughly intoxicating. "I want you," I murmured against his lips as I lightly ran my finger along his jawline and pulled him down to me a little bit more.

I could feel his hands running down my back and then he pulled away and started laughing, shaking his head as he took my hands into his.

"What's so funny?" I blinked at him confused.

"We need to stop or I'm not going to be responsible for my actions." He pressed his hand into the small of my back. "Let's go."

"Okay." I nodded, eager to leave. "We can take the C train I think."

"We're not taking the train baby, we're going to Uber." He growled at me. "I don't have time to waste with the MTA." His fingers squeezed my ass and I about melted. "Just hold on a second, I have to grab my gear, okay?"

"Okay." I nodded as I licked my lips and ran my hands down the front of my dress to smooth it down.

"Don't move," he said as he stared at my lips. "And don't go talking to any strange men." He cracked a smile, but his face looked serious as his eyes gazed into mine. I wasn't sure if I should feel happy that he didn't want me speaking to other guys or annoyed that he thought he could be so possessive when I owed him nothing. I decided to ignore it and as he walked away, I pulled my lip gloss out of my handbag and reapplied it quickly.

"*W*hich way to your bedroom?" He groaned as we stumbled through my front door. He was unbuttoning his shirt as I slipped my high heels off and slammed the door shut.

"Do you want to check on Frosty first?" I giggled as he threw his shirt on the ground.

"Frosty's fast asleep dreaming of a big juicy steak," he said as he shook his head and I watched as he unbuckled the top of his jeans. "Come here, sexy." He grabbed a hold of my hands and pulled me toward him and then he buried his head between my breasts and kissed my chest. "I've been wanting to do this since I saw you in that sexy dress." His fingers reached up and started moving the thin straps of my dress down. My breath caught as his fingers grazed my skin, making me tremble with sweet anticipation for what was going to come next.

"Oh yeah?" I said and my hands reached to his jeans and undid the zipper. "I've been wanting to do this all night as well," I said and then pulled his jeans down. He stepped back from me and pulled them off completely so that he was just standing there in a pair of black boxer briefs, his manhood very evidently excited to see me.

"Come here," he said and then motioned for me to lift my arms up. He reached down to the hem at the bottom of my dress and pulled it up in one swift movement. When it got to my hips I had to wiggle around a little bit as it was a bit tight on me and I felt a little bit self-conscious that it didn't slide off easily, but then I saw the look of desire on his face, and I realized that he hadn't noticed or didn't care that the dress didn't fit me that well. As he pulled the dress over my fingertips and threw it to the ground, he started to whistle and lick his lips like some sort of hungry wolf. "Are you a Victoria's secret model and didn't tell me?" he said as he ran his fingers down my stomach gently.

He stared at my naked body and his eyes were dark and veiled as he looked back at me. "Bedroom?" He grunted and I took his hand and led him toward my room. As soon as we reached my door, he grabbed me, pulled me into his arms and carried me to the bed. He dropped me onto the mattress and then jumped up next to me quickly.

His mouth quickly found mine and we started kissing passionately, our bodies intertwining as our legs linked together. My breasts crushed against his chest and his light splattering of hairs tickled my nipples. I moaned against his lips as his fingers found their way between my legs and rubbed me gently. I squirmed underneath his touch and he groaned into my ear. His hands continued to play with me and my body felt like it was on fire. I reached down to touch his hardness and he clutched me to him tighter. His cock felt like it was thick and long and I was excited to see it in the flesh. I pushed him so that he was lying flat on his back and then I scrambled to make my way on top of him so that I was straddling him. His hardness was between my legs now and I moved back and forth gently as I looked down at him.

He gazed up at me with narrowed eyes and his hands reached up to play with my breasts. I leaned down to trail my hair across his chest and licked his belly button. I felt his intake of breath as I kissed lower and my mouth covered his cock through the fabric and sucked lightly. His body went incredibly still and I just smiled to myself at his reaction. I waited a few seconds before I pulled his briefs off and threw them on the floor, not caring where they landed and then I looked at his manhood. He was already really hard, and I swallowed quickly thinking about taking him inside of me. He would be the biggest guy I'd ever slept with, and I wondered if that meant he would be amazing in bed or if that meant he'd be lazy.

He knew he was hot, and he had a big cock, so it could mean that he was just out to get his. I shouldn't have worried though because within seconds he was pushing me back on the bed and pinning me down. This time he was on top of me and he was completely in control. His cock rested on my stomach and he leaned down to suck on my breasts. He kissed down my stomach until he was taking my panties off and I moaned as I felt his tongue gliding up my calf to my inner thigh.

"Do you taste as sweet as you smell?" His voice was hoarse as his mouth came into contact with my woman-hood and licked and sucked. I cried out as I felt his tongue entering me and I reached down and grabbed his hair, my eyes closed as my body concentrated on the multiple different frissons of passion that were running through me. He ate me as if he'd been starving for days and I was the only food he'd have for one more week. He devoured me like he couldn't get enough and my thighs trembled as they pushed into his face. I didn't want it to end; my orgasm was building so sweetly and I was close to coming, but I didn't want to lose the warm soft touch of him inside of me and then he withdrew his tongue and I cried out loudly. "Carter," I almost screamed as he jumped off of the bed.

"Sh," he said as he ran through my bedroom door. "My wallet's in my jeans," he said as he ran and I knew what that meant. The condoms were in his wallet. I was glad that he was thinking because at that moment the last thing on my mind had been protection. I felt slightly ashamed and annoyed with myself. I was too smart to not have remembered to ask him to use a condom, but I blamed it on the alcohol and ecstasy running through my body. Before I could beat myself up anymore he was running back into the bedroom with a huge grin on my face.

"I got it," he said as he jumped onto the bed and I couldn't stop myself from laughing at him as he ripped the packet open.

"Careful big boy," I teased him and he just grinned. I watched him throw the wrapper to the side and then he slid the condom down onto his still very hard and very large penis. It must have been about seven inches and pretty solid. Very nice.

"Come here." He pulled me toward him and kissed me, his hand sliding between my legs and two fingers finding their way inside of me.

"Oh," I cried and fell toward him, kissing his shoulder and biting down into his skin. He pushed me back on the mattress and hovered over me. I watched as he reached down and positioned himself at my opening. "I know you won't believe me but I usually don't do things like this." I gasped as he pushed the tip of his cock inside of me.

"Sh," he said and then I felt him thrusting into me in one clean stroke.

"Oh," I cried out as I felt him deep inside of me. He moved in and out of me slowly at first and I reached up and ran my fingers down his chest, my nails digging into his skin.

"You like that?" he whispered into my ear, as he thrust into me again, this time with more force.

"Yes," I cried out as he moved back and forth. My legs tightened around his waist and I felt his body shudder slightly as I squeezed my inner thigh muscles in. He started moving faster then and I could barely believe how great it felt. He felt amazing inside of me and when he finally came, I felt his fingers on me and I came just seconds later. He collapsed on the bed next to me and grinned.

"Give me five minutes and we can do another room."

"Another room?"

"You said you wanted the first time to be in the bed. I assume that meant you wanted me to fuck you all over your apartment?"

"Oh really?" I smiled at him lazily, my finger running down his chest. "Where would you have us doing it next?"

"I wouldn't mind you riding me on the couch." He winked at me. "I like it when a woman is on top and you seem like a woman that likes to be in control."

"You want me to ride you?" I was starting to feel horny again already.

"I want you to ride me like you're a jockey at the rodeo."

"Jockey at the rodeo?" I started laughing. "I don't think they have jockeys at rodeos? Jockeys are in horse races. Rodeos are for bull riding and cattle steering and stuff."

"Ride me like a cowgirl on a bull then." He caught my finger and brought it to his mouth and sucked on it. "Ride me like I'm the biggest bull you've ever seen."

"You are the biggest bull I've ever seen." I gasped as his fingers pinched my nipples.

"And so I assume I'm biggest that you've ever had?" he questioned, his eyes intense on my face.

"Do you really want to know the answer to that?" I swallowed hard as he lowered his lips to my nipple and started nibbling. "Oh, Carter," I moaned. "Don't stop."

"You want me again, don't you, Lila?"

"Yes," I groaned.

"Am I the biggest you've ever had?" He grunted, and he looked up at me. I stared back down at him and his eyes were veiled. He had a cocky smile on his face and I knew he already knew the answer. It wasn't even that he was big, it was that he was big and thick and knew exactly how to move it. He was a skilled lover. A very skilled lover.

"Carter." I shook my head at him and he growled and he licked down to my belly button and then went even lower, bringing me to ecstasy once again.

~

"So, Lila, tell me about yourself." Carter played with my hair as we lay back in the bed lazily.

"What do you want to know?" I yawned, feeling tired, but not wanting to go to sleep yet. I was the most satiated that I'd ever felt in my life. We'd had sex three times, and I was absolutely exhausted. Happy, but exhausted.

"Who are your favorite musicians?" he asked with a gleam in his eyes.

"I like The Strokes," I said trying to think of the coolest band I listened to, but not being able to come up with anything other than them.

"Oh, their song 'Last Nite' is cool." He started humming something I didn't recognize, and he shook his head. "I think that's one of their most popular songs, right?"

"Um, I'm not good with lyrics and song names," I said honestly. "I'm awful at karaoke."

"But they have the words on the screen."

"And I still get them wrong." I made a face as I rested my head on his chest, his fingers still playing in my hair.

"Oh Lila." He laughed. "Who are your real favorites?"

"I don't want to say." I laughed. "You'll make fun of me."

"No I won't."

"Do you want a glass of water?" I asked him. "You must be thirsty."

"No water, I want to know who your favorite musician is."

"Ed . . ." My voice trailed off as I looked up at his gleaming eyes, he was now grinning uncontrollably. "What?"

"I know who you're going to say."

"No, you don't."

"Yes I do."

"No, you, don't."

"I'm in love with the shape of you . . ." he started singing and his hand ran down my bare back to my ass. "Push and pull like a . . ."

"Okay, okay." I groaned. "You got me. I love Ed Sheeran."

"You were right by the way."

"Right about what?"

"I'm totally judging you."

"Whatever!" I laughed. "I'm guessing he's not on your playlist."

"He's not on my playlist, no." He winked at me. "Are you into Bieber as well?"

"Ed Sheeran is not the same as Justin Bieber." I poked him in his muscular taut stomach.

"Oh, I forgot, sorry. Pop is pop to me."

"Don't be a hater."

"I'm not a hater." He laughed and then he pulled me up so that my face was next to his. "Well, maybe just a little bit," he said before he kissed me on the lips. "I'm not saying he's not talented . . ." His voice trailed off, and I hit him lightly in the shoulder.

"Carter Stevens, sh," I said and as I closed my eyes to just enjoy the moment, I realized how surreal the whole moment was. "Do you know that we just met?"

"I think I know that." I could hear the smile in his voice. "I was there."

"Do you think this is weird?" I asked, but weird wasn't the word I wanted to use. I wanted to ask him if he thought I was easy, but I didn't know that I wanted his answer. I loved his honesty, but sometimes you didn't always want honesty.

"Not for me," he said as he kissed the top of my head. "But I guess as a musician I meet attractive women and know that if I want something to happen I have to act then and there or I might never see them again."

"Yeah," I mumbled, not really wanting to hear about how this was an everyday occurrence for him. I mean, I knew we weren't headed to the altar, but he didn't need to shove it in my face, how unspecial I was.

"I guess you've never really had a one-night stand before, huh?" je said and I stilled. Was this it then? Were we only going to have this one night? Not that I cared, of course, but it would have been nice to have seen him and slept with him a few more times, but then I supposed what would that make him to me? My booty call? A friend with benefits? Would it even be considered friends with benefits if we weren't even friends? And did I want that? Not really. I didn't want to get into any long-term casual sex relationship. I mean it was all good and well to have some fun, but I didn't think friends with benefits ever went well for anyone.

"No, not really," I said honestly. "I've not slept with loads of guys and most were in relationships with me."

"Most?" he said questioningly.

"There was one guy." I sighed, thinking back to my college days. "I thought we were in a relationship, he didn't, we hooked up four times and then he started hooking up with my roommate."

"Ouch."

"Ouch, indeed." I laughed then. "It was my own fault, looking back at it now. He'd never once mentioned us being boyfriend and girlfriend. He never took me on any real dates. He bought me Wendy's one night, and I was over the moon. It really should have taken more than that to make me fall for him."

"So I take it you're not hung up on him then."

"No, not at all." I almost laughed. "To be honest and this might sound really bad, but I can't even remember his name."

"Oh, Lila." He laughed then and held me close to him. "You're funny. I'm glad you're funny."

"What would you have done if you found out I wasn't funny?"

"I'd leave."

"You'd just leave the bed?"

"Yup." He stroked my shoulder. "I'd jump out and be like see ya."

"Oh, wow."

"I don't normally spend the night," he said in a low tone.

"Oh?" I didn't question why he'd decided to stay the night with me.

"It's too intimate a gesture, and it makes a woman expect more," he said nonchalantly. "We're already on the same page, so it's okay."

"Yeah, it's fine," I said and kissed his chest. Just because it felt like paradise lying in his arms didn't mean we were meant to be together. "I'm glad you decided to stay."

"Me too," he said softly. "Me too." And then he stopped talking and within a few minutes I heard him snoring lightly, his chest rising beneath me. I smiled to myself as I listened to his heartbeat and then within a few seconds I was falling asleep myself.

~

I yawned as I walked into the kitchen at work. I needed caffeine and a bagel, preferably with cream cheese. The previous night had been amazing, but my body felt slightly sore and still very tired.

"Hey, Lila, you want to go for a drink after work?" My friend and work colleague Dante asked me as we stood there and made ourselves some coffees with the new Keurig machine that had been put in just a few weeks prior. "April says that El Ranchero has happy hour tonight." His hazel-green eyes sparkled as he tried to convince me to go out. I tried not to compare his eyes to Carters baby blues. For some reason I hadn't been able to stop thinking of Carter. Well, I knew the reason why, but it annoyed me slightly. I didn't want to be thinking about Carter.

"I should go home," I said, not really needing to go home straight after work, but I was hoping to see Carter in the hallway or something. I was not going to knock on his door. Or text him. Nope. If he wanted to talk to me, he could text me first. He has rushed out of the apartment quite early in the morning because he needed to walk Frosty and I hadn't seen or heard from him since.

"Why?" Dante looked surprised. "You don't want to get a drink?"

"I met a guy, well, kinda . . ." My voice trailed off. I didn't know what to say about Carter. "We hooked up."

"No way." Dante looked shocked. I knew he wasn't judging me because Dante was the king of random dates and hookups. He was most probably the second best looking man I knew, behind Carter. In fact some people might consider him a better catch than Carter. He's gorgeous, a partner at the firm and he's a millionaire, due to some family businesses he ran with his cousins. Dante and I had never dated, but I'd always thought he was cute. Not that I would ever hook up with a guy from work; you don't shit where you eat. I'd seen that from other people's disasters.

"Yes, way. He's a musician though and a playboy, so . . ." I didn't need to say more. Dante was very similar to Carter in that he also wasn't looking for a relationship. I wasn't sure why I was surrounded by men that were scared of commitment. I used to think it was something about me until I realized that men in general were pussies when it came to serious relationships. I really didn't understand what so many of them were afraid of. Was love really that bad?

"Don't even think about him. Let's go out for tequila shots."

"And guacamole?" I asked hopefully, capitulating easily.

"Yes and you'll have to tell me more about this wannabe." He laughed. "And I'll have to tell you about Nana and her plan for me."

"Oh, another plan?" I laughed already ready to laugh at whatever the story was. Dante's nana was always trying to hook him and his two cousins up. She wanted grandkids so badly and none of her grandsons were interested in getting married anytime soon.

"Yes, another girl." He rolled his eyes. "I don't know where she finds them."

"Oh, Dante. I don't know what to tell you." I heard my phone beeping, and I groaned. "That's my alarm. I've got to finish off these briefs to get to opposing counsel soon. Just email me the details for tonight."

"Sounds good. I should go as well. I have a meeting with Kaplan now. We're going to hire some new associates next month."

"Great," I said enthusiastically. Maybe I'd be able to work fewer hours if the firm hires more people. "Chat later," I said and walked back to my office. I looked at my phone and opened my messages and call log just to make sure I hadn't missed anything from Carter. There was nothing from him and I sighed as I put the phone down on my desk. I couldn't afford to develop a crush on him or have him in my head. Especially as it had only been a one-night stand as far as he'd been concerned. Though what a night it had been. I closed my eyes and pictured Carter's face between my legs and blushed. It wasn't that we'd done anything truly dirty or scandalous. It was more the fact that this time last week I didn't even know who he was. This time last week I didn't even know he existed and now, well, now he knew how to make me come in ways no other man had ever figured out. And I wasn't sure that one night was going to be enough for me.

"*D*oes That Make Me Crazy"

"*B*ro, you coming? Two dollar cans of Dos Equis." Chad stood at my doorway. "Me and the boys are headed out in ten." The boys being the other Harvard guys that had gone to college with Chad and now worked here at the J.D. Morganland with us.

"Okay, maybe." I nodded at him. "I need to figure out some sell prices for a client." I picked up the stack of folders and held them up to him just so he knew I could be here all night.

"Seth said that they got the girls wearing short tops now like at Hooters," Chad said still trying to convince me.

"We'll see, man." I dismissed him and returned to my files. I couldn't care less what price my clients sold their stocks at, but this was my job and I still needed to do my job until I got my bonus in a few weeks. Then I'd be handing in my notice and going full time as a musician. I was incredibly nervous, but super stoked and excited for this next step in my career. I picked up my calculator and then clicked on my keyboard to see the NASDAQ closing numbers. As the numbers piled onto the screen my mind thought back to the previous night with Lila. She'd been dynamite in bed; sexy, giving, beautiful. Everything had felt so warm and natural and her body had been perfection; warm and soft in all the right places. And when she'd straddled me on her couch and pretended to ride me like a cowgirl, I'd almost come right away. I'd been surprised when she'd woken me up at 3:00 a.m. to go at it again, but I hadn't complained. I looked at my phone and wondered if I should text her, but decided against it. I didn't want her thinking I was too eager. Girls always hated guys that texted too soon or too much. I knew that. I'd seen it with Danielle. Yeah, she complained when guys didn't text, but she had no respect for those that seemed too eager. I didn't want Lila to think I was too interested.

There was something about her that intrigued me. She was different than other women I'd met, and I didn't like that I couldn't read her. She wasn't clingy or trying to get me to commit to something that I didn't want, and while I appreciated that, a part of me was annoyed. Why did she think I wouldn't make a good boyfriend? I mean, I didn't want to be her boyfriend, but I didn't get why she thought I wouldn't be a good one. I'd given her the fuck of her life last night. That I knew for sure. The way her fingernails had dug into my skin, the way she'd been panting, the way the sweat on her skin glistened in the moonlight through her bedroom window. The way I could smell myself on her this morning. It had been hot as hell and I was growing hard just thinking about it. I put my phone down and jumped up. I didn't need to think about this girl. I didn't need any distractions.

"Hey, Chad," I shouted down the hallway as I got to my office door. "I'm done, let's go for those drinks." I'd worry about the files tomorrow. I couldn't concentrate right now. I just needed to get drunk and flirt with some hot girls in short tops.

~

"So, this chick comes up to me and she's like hey, aren't you dating my friend Olga." Chad is grinning as he tells his story. "And I'm like fuck, 'cause I'm with this girl Patsy that I'd just told that I hadn't gotten laid in a year."

"Shit." Brandon takes a chug of his beer. "So what did you say?"

"I said I had no idea who Olga was and went home and banged Patsy," Chad said and laughed. "Next day I called Olga and banged her too and then . . ." He paused for dramatic effect and I looked around the bar, feeling bored. How many stories could Chad tell us about how he dicked over women?

"What?" Brandon asked eagerly, eating it up. He was an intern, and I knew he was imagining that this would be his life once he graduated from college. "And then what?" he prodded.

"I got Olga and Patsy together and we had a three-some." Chad looked proud of himself and I just took a chug of beer. There was no way that I believed this story was true.

"Wow, cool." Brandon high-fived Chad and I was just about to say something when I heard a familiar laugh. I looked around the restaurant quickly to see if I could iden-tify the owner of the laugh. My breath caught as I saw Lila sitting at a table next to a tall guy in a suit; across from her sat another guy and a woman. All of them in suits. Lila was staring at the man next to her with wide laughing eyes. I frowned as I noticed her patting his shoulder and nodding along to something he was saying.

I felt inexplicably angry watching her sitting there drinking, looking like she was having the time of her life. Why wasn't she at work? Hadn't she been talking about how busy she was at the office. And why did she look so happy? We hadn't texted all day. I'd thought she would have been a little sad that she hadn't heard from me, given the night we'd just had. But maybe she had lied to me and this was something she did frequently. My eyes narrowed as I watched her throwing her head back and laughing even harder than before. Did she have a thing for this guy? Granted he was handsome in one of those dark Italian ways with his brunette hair and olive skin. Was that the type of guy she liked then? He couldn't have been further away from my golden blond hair and blue eyes. But he wasn't the one slamming into her last night.

"Yo, Stevens, want another one?" Chad's voice brought me back to the conversation, and I nodded.

"Yeah, man," I said and then because I could see no reason not to I decided to head over to go and chat with Lila. "I'll be right back, I think that I see a friend." And with that I walked over to Lila's table. "Hey, Lila," I said in a loud cheery voice as I approached their booth. "Fancy seeing you here!"

"Carter!" She looked at me in surprise and gave me a shy smile, and I was pretty sure she threw a guilty look toward the guy next to her. I could feel myself growing angry. Was she playing me and this fool?

"So who are your friends?" I asked looking around the table. "I'm Carter Stevens, by the way."

"Dante Vanderbilt." The guy next to me nodded at

me, a smile on his face. I hated him instantly as I noticed his Rolex. Rich prick. I looked away from him without acknowledging his outstretched hand and looked at the other two at the table.

"And you guys?"

"Sandi." An older looking lady beamed at me and fluttered her eyelids. She was about fifty-five, but she was still hot. I beamed back at her.

"Nice to make your acquaintance, Sandi."

"Ben." The other guy was nondescript in looks and from what I could tell, personality. No competition there.

"Surprised to see you here, Lila," I said as I turned back to look at her. "I thought you had a busy day today. At least that's what you said last night." I have a quick look to Dante so he could infer exactly what I meant by that comment and he just smirked. Asshole.

"I did have a busy day, but Dante convinced me to come out," she said with a smile still on her face.

"I see." I nodded and waited for her to ask me about my day or why I hadn't texted, but she didn't say anything. "So can my friends and I join you? We can make a party of it." And before they had time to respond I called out to Chad and Brandon and waved them over.

"Join us, why don't you?" Dante said in a smug voice and I looked over at him for a few seconds without saying anything. If Lila was hooking up with this jerk she was an idiot and had no taste.

"So how do you guys know each other?" I asked as Chad and Brandon approached.

"We all work at the firm together." Lila took a sip of her strawberry margarita.

"I see," I said and then I had to laugh at how crazy I was acting. "You look nice today, Lila."

"Thank you, Carter. You look nice as well." Her brown

eyes were warm as she looked at me. "I'm glad to see you made it into work," she teased me and all of a sudden my shoulders relaxed.

"Have you had dinner?" I asked her and then looked to see what dishes were on the table.

"No, I was going to cook when I got home."

"Oh yeah?" I raised an eyebrow at her, hoping for an invite. I didn't normally see women two nights in a row, but I'd excuse it this time for a nice home cooked meal.

"Yeah." She nodded, with no invitation extended.

"What are you cooking?"

"Quiche Lorraine with a salad."

"Yum," I said and licked my lips.

"I think he's hinting for an invite, Lila," Dante said and he laughed then as he chugged from his beer. "And quite obviously."

"Oh." Lila looked at me and blushed. "Did you want to come for dinner?"

"If it's not an inconvenience," I said as if I was some old Victorian gentleman. "Hey, can I chat with you for a second." I grabbed her hand and pulled her out of the booth. I placed my beer can on the table and walked toward the door holding her hand. We exited and then I turned toward her.

"What did you want to say?" she asked me curiously, and I just leaned forward and grabbed her face and started kissing her. She kissed me back and my hands ran up to cup her breasts through her blouse. "Carter." She shook her head and pulled back. "We're outside."

"So?" I said, but I took a step back. Was she concerned that Dante might see?

"In front of the restaurant on a busy street." She shook her head at me. "I'm not going to make out with you in front of the world."

"It's not like I'm asking you to fuck right here in daylight," I said feeling slightly annoyed.

"I never said you were." She shrugged. "I'm here with my workmates. It's just not professional for me to be here making out with you. They've never met you before. They've never even heard of you before. You're not my boyfriend. I don't want any questions."

"What sort of questions?" I asked, but I knew I was just being difficult. What she said made sense. I just didn't like it.

"You know what sort of questions. The *who is this guy* question and *how do you know him*." She sighed. "I don't really want to talk about my one-night stand with the world."

"Or your two-night stand," I said and winked at her.

"What does that mean?" she asked, her face going red. I laughed as I ran a finger down the side of her face.

"It means that tonight I'm going to show you how to have even more fun."

"Oh?" She blinked and then smiled at me. "How do you know I had fun last night?"

"By the way you screamed out my name." I watched as she blushed again. "It's a good thing that I'm your neighbor because you would have woken me up with all your crying out."

"Carter." She made a face at me. "Shh."

"Am I lying or am I telling the truth. Just a little bit harder, Carter, just a little bit deeper, yeah, that's how I like it, big boy."

"Stop." She hit me in the arm as she laughed. "I didn't say any of that."

"Exactly. Because I knew just what you needed without you having to tell me." I winked at her and felt myself warming as she giggled. I enjoyed watching her laugh, her face looked so beautiful and carefree as if she had no worries in the world.

"You're so full of yourself." She grabbed my hand. "Come on, let's finish our drinks and then we can go back."

"So eager." My heart was racing. I loved that she wasn't playing games. She wanted this as badly as I did. "We can just leave, I don't care about my beer."

"I can't just leave." She shook her head and dragged me toward the front door again. "Dante will wonder what happened." I held my groan in as she said his name. I didn't like the guy, but I wasn't going to tell Lila that; though a part of me wondered if I should warn her that he was likely trying to get into her pants so she should steer clear of him. I followed her back to the table and I could see Chad giving me a knowing look. I just ignored him and went to the bar to pay my tab. Then I walked back to the table where Lila was chatting with Dante.

"You ready?" I asked. "There's a train arriving in seven minutes that we can make if you hurry."

"Wow, you must be hungry." Lila's face held a trace of humor and I rubbed my stomach.

"Yeah, I haven't eaten since lunch. Let's go." I grabbed her hand and threw down two twenties on the table. "This is for Lila's share," I said and smirked at Dante. He wasn't the only one with money. Granted, I was about to be leaving my six figure a year job, but at least for now, I was a baller as well. And if I ever made it as a musician, I'd have more money than I'd know what to do with.

"You're a bit rude, you know that right?" Lila gasped as I made her run toward the station.

"How am I rude?"

"You can't just put money on the table and say let's go.

I was trying to make plans with Dante and I wasn't able to."

"What a pity." Like I cared.

"I just don't get you, Carter Stevens., she said as we ran down the steps. "I know I don't know you well, but I know Danielle quite well and she's so sweet and nice and you're . . ." Her voice trailed off as we went through the turnstile.

"And I'm what?"

"You're quite bullish," she said as we finally stopped to wait for the train that was going to arrive in two minutes.

"Bullish? Well, that's a new one." I pulled my phone out. "I guess what they say is true."

"What do they say?"

"You should really get to know someone before you sleep with them." I winked at her and she just groaned.

"You're too much."

"But you still want me."

"Maybe."

"Just maybe?" I looked at her thoughtfully. "Just maybe, huh?"

"Did I stutter?" She smiled.

"You're going to pay for that tonight?" My mind already trying to think of suitably dirty punishments that would have her begging me to take her.

"Oh yeah? Is that a threat?"

"No, it's a promise," I said, and the conversation was stopped by the arrival of our train.

"So tell me why you decided to become a lawyer," I asked her as we sat down. I was surprised to realize that I actually cared about her answer. I was genuinely interested in getting to know who she was. This was something new to me and I wondered if I was finally maturing or if this was because she actually had a career and the majority of women I hooked up with were wannabe models and actresses.

"I wanted to save the world." She made a face. "I used to watch these TV shows that made being a lawyer seem so glamorous and cool."

"And it's not like that?"

"No." She made a face and sighed. "When I went to law school, I had a bad feeling that I wasn't going to enjoy practicing law but I wasn't sure. I took some moot court classes, and that's when I realized I really didn't enjoy public speaking. I get really nervous being in front of large crowds." She shook her head. "So opposite to you, huh?"

"I get nervous sometimes, but yeah, not really. I love performing to large crowds. The larger the better. Where did you go to law school again?"

"University of Iowa." She winked at me. "Go Hawkeyes."

"Ugh."

"In heaven there is no beer, that's why we drink it here. And when we're gone from here, our friends will be drinking all our beer." She sang the Iowa victory song, and I groaned even louder.

"Corn lover."

"Hater." She laughed.

"So your family lives in Iowa?"

"Yes." She nodded. "I grew up in Des Moines, but went to Iowa for undergrad and law school."

"And then you moved to the big city?"

"Ha ha," She rolled her eyes at me. "I'm not some farm girl, you know. My dad is a policeman and my mom is a nurse."

"Nice, my dad is an accountant and my mom was a housewife," I said. "They're in Ohio, but I moved here for college."

"I heard. You went to Columbia?"

"Yup, bet you didn't think I was a smarty-pants, huh?"

"Nope," She grinned at me. "I never would have guessed you were smart. I'm still questioning it."

"Very funny."

"So tell me something else about you, Carter. What do you do for fun?"

"I like to write music. I want to release my own album with original songs," I said thinking about the band and my goals. "I also like to bowl. A lot."

"Oh yeah? Are you good?"

"Let's just say I took a class in college. I'll whip your ass." I looked at the sign as the train stopped. "Our stop is next."

"Yup." She nodded.

"Have you ever been to Chelsea Piers? They have a really cool bowling alley there."

"No, I've never been." She shook her head and then jumped up. "This is our stop."

"We should go sometime," I said as we walked off of the train and I saw the look of surprise on her face. "I mean if you can make the time."

"I didn't think you'd actually want to hang out with someone you're having a two-night stand with." She looked slightly embarrassed, and I wasn't exactly sure how to answer her. It wasn't normal for me to hang out with the women I hooked up with outside of the bedroom and I never invited them bowling. Bowling was sacred to me. It was one of my all-time favorite activities and I usually only went with my good friends.

"Well, just because we're having a two-night stand doesn't mean we can't also be friends." Not that I needed anymore friends.

"Yeah true," she said, and I watched as she took out a

couple of dollars from her handbag to give to an old man that was begging outside of the subway station.

"He's just going to buy alcohol," I said as we walked away.

"We don't know that. Maybe he's going to buy food. Maybe he's going to pay his rent."

"Maybe he's going to buy drugs or pay for his BMW."

"Carter, why are you so cynical." She gazed at me thoughtfully. "I'm the attorney. I should be the one doubting his intentions." And then she paused for a second. "And you know what, it was three dollars. It's for him to decide what he does with it. When you give charitably, you can't tell people what to do with the money. They do what is in their heart."

"Did you go to a catholic school by any chance?" I asked her as I looked at her earnest face, with her cute little nose up in the air.

"Huh? What?" She looked confused.

"You seem like such a Goody Two-Shoes with all your charity talk. I was curious if you went to catholic school."

"Carter Stevens, really? Really?" She opened the main door to the apartment building and then turned to me. "I didn't go to catholic school no, but we did go to church every other weekend when I was a kid."

"Oh no, are you going to try and convert me?"

"Convert you from what to what?"

"I don't know." I laughed as I followed her up the stairs. My eyes were focused on her shapely ass and I wanted to run my hands down it and squeeze, but I stopped myself.

"Well here we are," she said as she stopped outside of her apartment. "Are you going to come in?"

"You don't know how badly I want to *come* in." I winked at her and she groaned as I laughed. "But I should walk Frosty first. As that is the reason I'm here, after all."

"Oh, yes, poor little Frosty." She smiled. "Don't let me stop you. I'll change and start dinner and you should come over as soon as you can."

"Sounds good to me," I said and stepped forward and kissed her. "I'll be as quick as I can be."

"Okay." She smiled and unlocked her door. "I'll see you soon."

"See you soon," I said, and I stood there until she'd closed the door behind her. I rushed over to my own door and Frosty came running up to greet me as I walked in. "Hey, buddy boy," I said as I bent down to stroke his head. "Hold on, I'll take you on a walk in just a second. Let me just grab some water." I walked to the kitchen and Frosty followed me. "Talk about clingy." I laughed as he touched my leg. "I thought women were bad, but you take the cake, Frosty." He whined then, and I played with his ears before grabbing his leash. "Come on Frosty, let's go. If you're a good boy, I'll see if Lila will let you come over tonight as well." I didn't stop to question why I was so excited to get to Lila's place or why I felt like I was already missing her when I'd just seen her. "Frosty, I'm going to show her the time of her life tonight," I said as we headed out the door and down the stairs. As we passed Lila's front door, an idea for a song came to me and I started humming.

❧

"So I hope you like quiche." Lila moved back and forth in the kitchen cutting stuff up and I nodded.

"It smells great, as evidenced by Frosty's eager anticipation next to the oven." I pointed to the dog, his eyes were wide and anxious as if he knew that his chances of getting some of the quiche were slim to none. Maybe I'd sneak him a quick piece if he was a good boy.

"He's just so cute. I wish I had the time to get my own dog." She looked at Frosty wistfully and I wondered what else she wished she had.

"Thanks for letting me bring him over. I spoke to Danielle this morning, and she said he gets lonely in the evenings so I figured might as well let him hang with us."

"How is she? How's London?"

"She's good. Busy." I shrugged. "She loves her job, but I think they take advantage of her."

"Aw, that's rough."

"Yeah and it doesn't leave her much time to date. She's unlike us, I think she's ready for a serious relationship. My parents keep hinting for grandkids and thank God, she's the one getting all the calls."

"That sounds like Dante. His grandma is harassing him into getting married and having kids." She laughed, and I frowned as she brought up his name. Was she obsessed with this guy? Couldn't she talk about anything else?

"Anyway, I got the idea for a new song today." I changed the subject before she decided to continue going on about Dante. What sort of name was that?

"Oh yeah?" She gave me a look and I could have sworn that she'd laughed to herself before she spoke.

"Yeah, maybe I'll play it for you later."

"That would be cool." She shooed Frosty to the side so that she could open the oven door. And I watched as she put on an oven mitt so that she could pull the quiche out.

"Do you need my help with anything?" I said, realizing that I probably should have offered my services an hour ago as opposed to when the dinner was almost done. "I can wash up afterward if you like."

"I will not say no that." She giggled as she took a knife from her knife block and started to cut the quiche. "I hate to wash up."

"Well just look at us . . . two perfectly domesticated people," I said and then I jumped up and headed to the fridge when I realized what I'd said. "I'm getting another beer, want anything?"

"No, thanks," she said as if she hadn't noticed how awkward my last sentence was. Why did I use the word domesticated? I didn't even know I knew that word. I had no idea why I had used it. I was just here to get laid. "Frosty, come with me," I called out to my sister's greedy mutt as I made to leave the kitchen. "Do you mind if I turn the TV on? I'm curious to see what games are on tonight."

"Sure, and if you can't find anything I'm pretty sure *Grey's Anatomy* is on tonight."

"Sorry, what?" I blinked. "I don't know who Grey is and I sure don't want to see his anatomy."

"It's a TV show, silly, about a hospital."

"No thanks." I gave her my most winning smile. "That doesn't sound like anything I'd be interested in watching. Which reminds me of another reason why I'm glad we're not in a relationship. I don't have to suck it up and watch boring girly shows to be polite." She just stared back at me and rolled her eyes.

"And you wonder why you're such a catch," she mumbled under her breath, but it was loud enough for me to hear.

"Are you saying you don't think I'd be a catch?"

"You mean to anyone other than a sex-crazed vamp?" She cocked her head to the side.

"You don't like sex?" I was annoyed at her answer.

"I love sex, but if I was considering you for a real relationship I'd want more than just good sex."

"If you were considering me?" I raised an eyebrow up at her. "So you haven't even considered me?"

"Of course not." She took some plates out of the cupboard. "We both know you're not looking for a relationship and you're not relationship material either."

"Unlike Dante?" I snarled, starting to feel angry.

"What?"

"Do you think Dante is relationship material?" I didn't wait for her to answer. "That's a guy that just wants sex, I'm telling you. He wouldn't even come for dinner, he'd just be in the bed waiting and then he'd be gone."

"I don't think so." She shook her head. "Dante's a good guy."

"Uh-huh." I walked back into the kitchen and stopped in front of her. "Let me ask you this."

"Ask me what?"

"Have you already fucked him?"

"I know you didn't just ask me that?" Her jaw dropped and her eyes widened. "Really, Carter?"

"So?"

"Not that it's any of your business, but no. Dante is just me friend."

"Yeah?" All of a sudden I felt pleased. "That's good."

"You're crazy, dude." Her eyes stared into mine and for a few seconds I was scared she was going to ask me to leave.

"Maybe it's because of you. I remember, I remember when I lost my mind." I sang the Gnarls Barkley song and did a little dance and she started laughing. "I love the sound of your laugh," I said. "It's so infectious. You're always so happy."

"You haven't seen me at work." She grimaced and picked up both plates. "Grab the salad from the fridge and follow me."

"Oh, we're not eating in here?" I nodded toward her carefully made up table in the corner of the room.

"No, we're going to be naughty and watch TV and stuff our faces."

"Sounds good to me." I walked over to the fridge and grabbed a glass bowl filled with a very delicious looking salad. "Can I bring anything else over?"

"I have some French bread and butter but I'll get it. I need to slice the bread."

"You're spoiling me." I patted my stomach. "Or you're trying to get me fat so no other woman will want me."

"Yup, that's my plan." She giggled. "Follow me, Carter." And she proceeded to walk down the hallway to her living room. She placed the plates on her cherry wood coffee table and then switched on a lamp in the corner of the room. "Here's the remote," she said as she walked out of the room, and I settled down on her comfy white couch and flicked the TV on. I sat back and looked around the room while I waited for her cable box to come to life. She had two bookshelves on one side filled with stacks of books. Next to the shelves was a tall green plant. I had no idea what the plant was, but it looked cool. I looked to the other side and there was a large window overlooking the street, her curtains were open, but I supposed she was so high up that it didn't matter.

"What did you find?" She walked back into the room with a plate piled high with slices of a crusty looking baguette and a dish of butter.

"Nothing yet," I said. "This all looks very delicious by the way."

"Dig in," she said as she sat next to me. "I hope you enjoy it."

"Oh I will," I said and then placed the remote on the coffee table and went in for a kiss. Her eyes widened in surprise but she kissed me back passionately. My fingers went to the buttons on her shirt and I leaned forward to kiss her neck. "I think I'd like a special appetizer first though." I groaned as she reached down to massage my cock and I fell back as she started to undo my zipper.

"I think I'd like my appetizer first, actually." She winked and me and I just grinned up at her enjoying the sexy fun way she unbuttoned my shirt and kissed my chest. My whole body warmed as her lips touched my skin. Lila was someone different. Someone special. I knew that in my heart. I just didn't know if I was ready for someone like her in my life at this point.

"*B*lack Magic Woman"

I could hear my alarm ringing, but I didn't want to wake up. I was enclosed in Carter's warm strong arms and it felt like heaven. I didn't want to have to face reality and go to the firm, but I couldn't ignore the alarm any longer.

"I've got a gig later tonight." Carter kissed my cheek as soon as I opened my eyes. I blinked at him sleepily. He was staring down at me with a strange expression on his face and I wondered how long he'd been awake.

"Is that your way of telling me you need to leave so you can go and practice?"

"No." He grinned and kissed me on the lips this time. "It's my way of telling you I have a gig tonight."

"How long have you been awake?" I asked him suspiciously as I noticed he was surprisingly lucid for someone that had just woken up. I felt slightly self-conscious as my naked body pressed into his. My breasts were crushed against his chest and I could feel his manhood pressing into my belly intimately. I thought of all the things I'd done to his manhood the evening before and I blushed. I had given him a blow job as soon as I'd put the baguettes on the table and then he put me on all floors and entered me from behind so slowly and tantalizingly that I'd begged him to fuck me hard. I'd never used that kind of language before, but he just brought it out in me.

"About an hour," he said lazily as if it were no big deal and ran his hands through my wild mane.

"And you're still in bed?" My eyes widened in surprise. Had he been staring at me this whole time? And if so, what did that mean? "Don't you always practice in the morning? Do you need to go?"

"I wanted to look at your beautiful face, and I didn't want to disturb you from your beauty sleep." He reached over and touched my naked breast and played with my nipple. "Plus, I was hoping I'd get a reward for being a good boy."

"A reward?" I bit down on my lower lip and I could feel myself growing wet. For heaven's sake, I'd just woken up. I wasn't sure what had come over me.

"I want to feel myself inside of you again."

"Carter." I blushed. In the light of the cold sober day, I felt a little shy to hear his words. I still secretly loved how dirty he was, but the words still took me aback.

"What Lila?" He leaned forward and took my nipple in his mouth and tugged on it gently. "Don't you want a morning quickie?"

"I have to go to work, Carter." I moaned as I half-heartedly pushed him away and covered myself.

"Boo. It sucks that you have to rush to work." He made a face.

"Life of an attorney." I sighed, once again regretting my career choice.

"So are you going to come to my gig tonight?" he asked hopefully, his face resembling that of a little boy's asking Santa for a gift.

"You want me to?" I asked surprised. We'd already seen each other two nights in a row, I didn't think he'd want to see me again tonight. He'd made it dreadfully clear that he wasn't looking for a relationship or anything serious. In fact, he'd gone on and on about women becoming too attached to him too quickly. Hadn't he said that he liked to see a girl once a week and no more than that.

"Yeah, I want you to come." He sat up in the bed then and brushed back his hair. It was growing out and was slightly too long at the front now. It covered his eyes every time it fell forward, and it made him look younger somehow. "So will you?" he asked again softly and if I hadn't known him better, I would have thought there was uncertainty in his tone. But there was no way that Carter Stevens was uncertain about anything.

"I'll try," I said. "I'm not sure if I'll be able to make it. What time do you guys go on?"

"Eight." He pulled the sheet down so that it was no longer covering my breasts or any part of my body. "You're so damn sexy, you know that, right?" His words warmed me, but a part of me wanted to hear more than that. I wanted our conversations to be more in-depth, though I wasn't sure that that would ever happen.

"Do you have time to listen to the new song that I wrote?" He stretched, and I watched as his muscles rippled. I smiled at the dark tan of his arms as they contrasted against his much fairer and paler chest. "What's so funny?" His eyes narrowed as he gazed at me. "You don't want to hear it?"

"No, I'd love to hear it," I said and sat up. I leaned over and gave him a kiss. "Play it for me."

"Go and shower," he said after he kissed me back. "I'll get some breakfast together and walk Frosty quickly. Then I'll grab my guitar and you can eat while I play."

"Yes, boss," I said, and he laughed.

"You can call me boss any day." He jumped out of the bed and I watched as he walked across the room, his naked butt firm and delicious. I couldn't stop my eyes from devouring him as he turned around and came back toward the bed. "Why are you still in bed?" He stood there in front of me and I looked down and saw his member saluting me, already somewhat hard.

"Um just watching you," I said, loving the way his eyes were staring at my breasts intently. I watched as he swallowed and then shifted his weight.

"Out of bed." He reached for my hands and pulled me up.

"I'm not ready yet." I yawned but got out at his insistence. "Just because you're ready doesn't mean I am."

"If you're going to get your work done and have time to watch me tonight, you need to make sure you get into work on time," he said in a stern voice and I tried not to roll my eyes at him. Since when had he become so responsible? And since when did he care? He pulled me toward him so that I was standing with my body pressed up against him. I looked up at his handsome face and my heart melted slightly. He was just so good looking. It wasn't even fair.

"Fine, fine," I said and ran my fingers down his chest. "I'm going to go in the shower now and I'm going to try to make it tonight, okay?"

"Okay." He nodded. "I'd really love it if you came," he said, his blue eyes bright. "It would mean a lot to me."

"Okay," I said and pulled away from him and walked over to my closet. I wanted to ask him why it would mean a lot to him. I wanted to ask him what he meant by that. Why did he care if I came or not? Did it mean he was falling for me? Or did he just like to have a lot of groupies around? I tried to remember what Danielle had told me about him, but I couldn't remember. I wanted to ask her more about him, but she was in England, plus he was her brother. The brother she'd warned me about. I wasn't sure what she would think if I called her and started giving her the fifth degree about his dating history.

I couldn't believe that I was falling for him. It wasn't that he was perfect. He was far from perfect, but there was a vulnerability about him that drew me to him in a way I'd never been drawn into any other guy. It was unexpected because he was so handsome and so talented. He was a frigging rock musician for heaven's sake, he could have any girl he wanted. He could be the cockiest most arrogant bastard and still get away with it, but there was a softness and a kindness behind his mask. He was a good guy even though he desperately tried to portray a different persona.

~

"*D*ante, hurry up, we're going to be late." I tugged on his shirt as he stood looking at his phone. I stared at my watch, and I sighed. We were already thirty minutes late. I didn't want to miss Carter's whole set.

"I'm just texting Kate and Sarah to let them know where we're going to be. They want to meet lover boy as well."

"Dante." I made a face at him. "Do not say anything like that around him!"

"Would I dare?" He laughed. "That guy is an asshole if I ever saw one."

"He's not an asshole."

"You're only saying that because you're sleeping with him but trust me. I know an asshole when I see one." He smirked at me. "I would know one because I am one."

"Uh-huh." I rolled my eyes at him. "One day you're going to meet Ms. Right and she's going to knock you off of your feet and you're not going to know what happened."

"I'd like to see that." His hazel-green eyes looked at mine with a devious look. "Never going to happen."

"Where are they? We're so late."

"Lover boy going to be upset?"

"No." I shook my head. "I told him that I wasn't sure if I could come . . ." I pulled out my phone to check my texts. I smiled when I saw Carter's name on the top of the screen. *Going on now, hope to see you.* It had also made me smile when I'd received it, and it made me smile now. I hadn't responded because I'd wanted to surprise him, but now I was nervous that I was going to be so late that I wouldn't get to see him perform at all.

"They will be here in five minutes," he said and put his phone in his pocket. He then looked into my eyes for a few seconds with a very pensive look, and I could tell that he wanted to tell me something.

"What's up?"

"I don't know whether or not I should say this. It's not really my place, but . . ." His voice trailed off as he looked at me thoughtfully.

"What, Dante?"

"I'd be careful around this guy," he said finally. "I don't know his intentions or where he's coming from, but he seems like he's all over the place and I think you can do better."

"Oh my God, he's just a hookup." I sighed, my face turning red as I knew in my heart that it was becoming more than just a hookup for me. "He doesn't have any intentions because he's told me that he only likes to have fun and that's fine because that's what I'm after as well."

"So why are we going to his show? And why are you worried we'll be late?"

"Well, I'm not worried we'll be late, because we're already late. I'm worried we'll miss the entire show."

"Who cares?" He made a face. "None of my hookups have invited me to come to see anything."

"Really? They haven't invited you or you haven't wanted to go."

"Touché." He laughed and put his hands up. "I'm just saying you're awfully defensive for someone in a no-strings attached relationship. I'd just be careful. I don't want to see you getting hurt." He put his hands on my shoulders and looked me in the eyes. "You're a beautiful girl inside and out and I want to make sure you meet the right guy. Because honestly, if I really thought you were the sort of girl that was interested in a hookup I would have set you up with one of my cousins."

"Which one? Blake or Steele?" I pretended like I was considering it and we both laughed.

"Oh Lila," he said. "What am I going to do with you?"

"Hurry into the show with me?" I asked hopefully, and he laughed and then pulled out his phone again.

"Okay, they have two more minutes. If they're not here, we will just head in."

"I don't see why we had to wait on them before we could go inside." I moaned. "I mean they're grown adults.

They're lawyers for frigging sake. They can't go to a rock show by themselves."

"Now, now, Lila," Dante said, but I just rolled my eyes. He had to know I was right. I knew that the other reason we were waiting was because Dante was hoping to hook up with one of them tonight, but he didn't want to be alone with either one of them. He wasn't that interested in making it a one-on-one date but interested enough to make it a "we stumble back to my place after the show" kinda night. He could talk about Carter all he wanted, but he was just as big a player. "Here they are." He pointed to two women walking toward us and I let out a breath I didn't know I'd been holding.

"Finally, oh my God. Let's go." And with that I started walking toward the bar, reaching into my handbag while I walked so that I could have my ID ready as soon as I hit the front entrance. My heart started racing with excitement as we got closer to the bar. I didn't even say hello to my friends or wait for them to catch up with us before I started heading toward the door. I was about five yards away when I started to feel guilty and stopped. I looked back and saw that they were all running to catch up with me, Dante leading the pack with a huge grin on his face. As they reached me, Dante gave me a wink.

"Not interested in this guy at all, are you?" he said, and before I could answer he had walked in front of me and was handing his ID to the bouncer and walking into the bar.

"Hey, Lila," the girls chorused in unison.

"Hey, Kate, hey, Sarah. Sorry for the rush, I just didn't want us to miss the show."

"New boyfriend?" Kate asked me with keen eyes.

"No, just a friend," I said. A friend I'm boinking, I

thought to myself. And really could I even call him a friend? Were we friends? We'd known each other less than a week. I mean I guess we were kinda friends. I think we both liked spending time with each other outside of the sex. We laughed a lot, and I really felt like he was interested in getting to know me as a person. I don't know why he cared or if he really did, but it felt nice to have someone ask me questions about myself. That hadn't happened in a while. Most of the guys that I met only talked about themselves.

"Oh, okay." Kate looked disappointed. She was most probably hoping that she could go back to the office and gossip about me with the other associates.

"Their band is great. You'll love them," I said as I handed my ID to the bouncer and hurried inside. The room was darkly lit, but my eyes soon adjusted to the light. The stage was dead center at the front of the room and there stood Carter, tall, dark, and handsome singing his heart out to some song I'd never heard before. I stood next to Dante as we waited for the girls to make it in, and I grinned at Carter and gave him a huge wave as his eyes made his way toward me. He looked at me for a few seconds, then at Dante and then continued surveying the room without acknowledging my smile or wave at all. Maybe he hadn't seen me? He continued to sing, and I grabbed Dante's arm and dragged him to the front of the crowd so that we could be dead and center in front of Carter.

"Can we get a drink first?" Dante said as he looked around the room. The place was packed with people that looked like they were all in their early twenties. "I'm going to need it to get through the night."

"Fine, come on." I looked around for the bar and started walking to the side of the room.

"Shall we do shots?" Kate said as she and Sarah caught up to us.

"No," I said as soon as Dante said, "Yes."

"Fine." I groaned. "But I'm only doing one shot."

"I'm ordering double shots of tequila and vodka and Sprites for everyone," Dante said as he called the bartender over. And of course, she came right away. I guess that was the power of being a tall, handsome man when it came to female bartenders.

"Fine," I said, but I wasn't really paying attention. I looked toward the front of the stage again, and my eyes met Carter's, but he looked away as soon as we made contact. What was up with him? I looked over to Sarah, who was dancing along to the song playing and grinning.

"Thanks for inviting me tonight," Sarah said. "This is awesome."

"I'm glad you could make it. The band is great."

"What's their name?"

"The Bedroom Rockers," I said and I couldn't stop myself from laughing. It was such a suitable name for a band Carter was in. He certainly rocked my world in the bedroom.

"Okay, don't look now, but the lead singer is totally checking you out," Sarah said with a huge grin. I could hear Carter singing Santana's "Black Magic Woman" through the speakers. "Got a black magic woman, Got me so blind I can't see . . ." The words were raspy as he sang and I wondered if he had chosen the song on purpose.

"Oh, yeah?" I said and looked toward the stage again because I had absolutely no chill. As soon as I looked toward the stage, I saw Carter singing to some girl standing in the front of the crowd. My eyes narrowed as I looked to see what she looked like. My breath caught as I saw her face, she was beautiful, with long black hair, and deep red lips. She was wearing a very revealing red dress and I could feel myself flushing with something akin to jealousy. I looked away and back toward the bar. I was not going to let Carter make me feel jealous.

"Ready for a shot?" Dante asked, his eyes watching me carefully. He could sense that my mood had changed slightly.

"Yes!" I almost shouted. "Bring it on." I waited for Dante to hand me my shot and I heard Carter speaking to the crowd.

"We're going to be taking a small break, folks, enjoy the music and our next set will start up again in fifteen minutes." I didn't look back to the stage to watch him getting off. I didn't want to see him flirting with that girl. And I didn't want him to think that I'd come here for him. Well, it was obvious I had come to the show to see him, but I didn't need him to know how upset I was feeling right now. He didn't owe me anything. I wasn't his girlfriend. He didn't need to acknowledge me.

"Can I get a whiskey on the rocks?" I heard Carter's voice behind me before I saw him. I looked over my shoulder and saw he was standing at the bar. I looked away, my skin feeling hot and bothered as I realized he had gone to the bar instead of coming to say hi to me. Had he not seen me? Was he mad at me? Why had he texted me to come if he wasn't going to say hi? "Lila?" I felt a hand tapping on my shoulder and turned around and saw Carter was now directly behind me. He had a small smile on his face but it didn't reach his eyes. His blue eyes looked slightly angry and annoyed, and I wondered what had happened to him.

"Hey, how's it going?" I said as I smiled at him widely. I didn't want him to think he had affected me in any way. "You guys rock."

"You didn't really hear much though, did you?" He looked at Dante, Kate, and Sarah. "You guys just got here. Where were you before this?"

"Oh, Dante and I just got a drink at this cute Italian place and then we were waiting for Kate and Sarah." I gestured to the two women who were staring at us in interest. "Kate and Sarah, meet Carter, the lead singer of the band."

"Hi, Carter." Kate grinned at him, but he just gave her a slight nod of his head.

"Had fun getting your drink?" he asked, his eyes accusing.

"Sorry, what?" I blinked up at him.

"I assume you had fun getting your drink with Dante?" He nodded toward Dante who was standing at the bar gazing at us with narrowed eyes. He gave me a look to ask if I was okay, and I nodded slightly.

"Yeah, we had fun. He's my friend, Carter."

"Friend, yeah right." Carter looked pissed. "I already told you what I think."

"We just wanted to come out and support you tonight."

"Does he know you were in my bed last night?" He hissed.

"Well, technically you were in my bed," I joked, trying to lighten the mood, but Carter didn't laugh. "Frosty ate the quiche we left on the table, by the way. I noticed the whole dish was empty this morning. Hopefully, he didn't get sick." I tried to change the subject, but Carter wasn't having any of it.

"Well, I have to start getting ready to go back on stage again," he said as he took a long gulp of his whiskey. "I'll talk to you after the show."

"This is really ridiculous, Carter," I said with a frown. I really didn't appreciate him treating me so coldly for reasons that made no sense, given our situation. "You're really just a totally moody, grumpy, asshole, aren't you?"

"Who are you to call me moody and grumpy?" His eyes bore into mine and he looked like a petulant little boy.

"Carter, listen to yourself."

"I don't have time for this right now. We'll talk after the show." And with that he headed back to the stage, his black jeans clinging to his muscular legs in ways that made him look even sexier than ever. I tried to ignore the fact that I still found him to be the most gorgeous and compelling man I'd ever met. I hated his mood swings, and I hated how he just jumped to conclusions. A fling shouldn't be so complicated. It should be fun, but maybe I was slowly coming to realize that I didn't want a fling with him. I'd never really wanted one and now I remembered why.

～

"The show was, absolutely, amazing," I praised Carter as he packed his guitar into a case in the backroom of the bar. "You really are so talented."

"Thanks." He nodded his back to me. "I see your friends left before we ended the last set."

"They needed to get up early tomorrow." I walked over to him. "Are you mad at me?"

"Why would I be mad at you?" He shook his head as he glimpsed at me briefly. "If you want to go have drinks and gallivant around town with some douchebag that obviously wants to fuck you, then that's up to you."

"Really, Carter?"

"My piece of advice though?" He paused and stood up straight to look at me. "I'd make sure to do an STD test first to make sure he's clean. He looks like the sort to have all sorts of diseases."

"Really, Carter?" My jaw dropped. "You're such a bloody asshole. How dare you? I have already told you that Dante and I are just friends. He actually was warning me about seeing you."

"Surprise, surprise." He snorted. "Of course he was."

"It's not like that. He just wanted to make sure I wasn't hooking up with a douchebag, turns out he had reason to be concerned."

"You weren't so concerned when I was going down on you last night. In fact, I seem to remember you begging me not to stop."

I just stared at him as he spoke, his mouth thin and his nostrils flaring. His eyes looked slightly cold, and I took a step back from him.

"I don't like you right now," I said as I shook my head. "I came out to your show to support you and have some fun, but you're being an absolute dick and I'm not going to let you talk to me that way."

"Am I lying though?" he asked, but he looked taken aback. "That's just really unprofessional of you to be hanging out with workmates wearing skimpy clothes and flirting and stuff. He is going to think you're up for the taking, even if you're not interested in that. Just because you're just being friendly doesn't mean he's going to see it that way." His voice was softer. "You have to understand where I'm coming from. I'm not trying to be a dick."

"Carter." I just shook my head. "If you listened to yourself, you would realize that you're making no sense, and, in fact, I find you to be very insulting right now. I think I'm just going to leave."

"I can get us an Uber back," he said hopefully as he tried to reach out to touch my hair.

"No thanks. I think I just want to go home by myself tonight."

"Okay," he said. "I'm sorry if I hurt you or said something I shouldn't have. I just like to be honest though I know most people can't handle the brutal truth."

"Carter Stevens, you do not know me at all." I sighed. "Look, what we had was fun, but maybe we should just leave it at the two nights and both of us can just move on."

"Is that what you want?" His mouth thinned and his eyes darted back and forth on my face. "Fine," he said as he turned away from me. He hadn't even waited for me to respond. "Fine, have a great night, Lila. Thanks for coming to the show. I hope you and your friends had a good night."

And with that, he turned back to his guitar and started fiddling around. I wanted to ask him what his problem was. I wanted to ask him why he was the way he was. It just didn't make sense to me. All this drama and jealousy, well, I assumed it was jealousy, and he didn't even want a relationship. I was so confused and upset I didn't know what to think. I walked out of the room without saying anything and left the bar with my head high. I wanted to cry, but I was not going to allow myself to give in to the feeling. Instead, I decided to walk a little while and just think.

I pulled out my phone and checked the world clock to see what time it was in London. I knew I shouldn't, but I had to speak to Danielle. She was the only one that would be able to give me some sort of clarity as to what was going on with Carter, because even if we never hooked up again, we would be living next door to each other for the next month, and I didn't want it to be awkward.

"*O*h, Lila." Danielle's voice was warm as she spoke to me. "I did try to warn you."

"I know." I groaned. "I didn't expect this to happen. He's just so confusing."

"My brother is a doofus." She groaned. "I'm going to be honest here, it sounds like he's reeking of jealousy." And then she laughed. "Sorry, I know it's not funny, but I've never seen him jealous before. Good on you."

"I wasn't trying to make him jealous though. Dante really is just my friend. We like to hang out after work." I sighed. "And anyway, Carter is the one that made it plain to me that he was only interested in a hookup because he needs to concentrate on his career as a musician."

"He takes himself way too seriously." Danielle's voice was dry. "I'm not sure who he thinks he is. Yes, he can sing, but he's no Freddy Mercury."

"Oh, Danielle." I laughed. "That's horrible."

"It's true. I have no idea why he thinks it's a good idea to quit his job, but that's on him. He better not try to move in with me. Trust me, he's just acting like a jealous fool."

"Why would he be jealous though?" I kind of wanted him to be jealous, but not if it was for the wrong reasons. "Do you think he likes me or do you think he's just scared he'll lose the attention that I give him?"

"Girl, if I knew how to understand men I would be a millionaire. Scratch that, I'd be a billionaire," Danielle said, and I laughed. "Look, here's what I can tell you about Carter, he's not a bad guy. He's my brother, and I love him, and he has his faults, but he's not a bad guy. He's not one of those guys that's a jerk because he had his heart broken either. He's been in relationships before but none of them were ever that serious. He's really always been about having fun and jamming. I suppose he's seen friends getting their hearts broken by girls in college and stuff, but I don't think he's ever gone through it himself."

"Really?" I was surprised by her statement. I'd totally assumed that he was an asshole because he'd been hurt in the past. "Never?"

"Look he's been in shitty relationships. I remember this one girl he dated, Elizabeth was her name. She was a huge bitch and totally played him, but he didn't love her. His ego was hurt, but he wasn't lying around the house crying, if you know what I mean?"

"Yeah, I guess so." I didn't know what to think of that. I didn't feel like I was any closer to getting to know or understanding Carter than I had been before the call.

"My brother is an enigma that even I don't understand. He's the reason I know that the saying *men are from Venus and women are from Mars* is true."

"Ugh, I just wish I could figure him out. I mean if he only wants a hookup why would he care if I was flirting with or sleeping with Dante?"

"Because men are weird." She sighed. "Look I don't mean to say this, but maybe try to talk to him and see how he feels."

"No way, we don't even know each other. This is all so weird."

"Sometimes people have instant chemistry and a connection that can't be explained. Maybe the love spell has hit him and he doesn't know what to do or feel."

"Oh, Danielle, who knew you were such a romantic. There's no way he's in love with me."

"You like him though, don't you?"

"Is it that obvious?"

"Maybe not, but you never would have called me in England if you weren't pining for him in some way."

"I'm sorry to bother you. I know it's early."

"It's no bother, Lila. You can call me at any time even if it's about my obnoxious brother."

"He's a nice guy underneath it all." I laughed. "He is obnoxious and easily angered, but he can also be sweet."

"And this is when I say I have to go," she said quickly. "I don't want you to start telling me how good he is in bed."

"I wouldn't talk about that," I lied. I would totally tell her how much of an expert he was with all parts of his body if I thought she'd be interested in hearing about it.

"I'll let you go."

"Keep me updated, Lila," she said before we hung up and I stood there standing in the middle of the street with my phone in my hand wondering what to do next. I wanted to go home, but I didn't want to be close to Carter. I was nervous I'd knock on his door and demand to know what was up. He couldn't just talk to me like that and get away with it. It was so totally uncool. And he hadn't even apologized. It was like he didn't even get it. I sighed as I realized I couldn't just stand in the street thinking and decided to hail an Uber. I had to go home. I'd just have to have some self-control.

❧

I walked up the stairs slowly and my heart stopped when I saw Carter standing outside my door.

"You're home," he said with a sheepish smile and some yellow sunflowers in his hand.

"I'm home." I nodded as I headed toward my door.

"I was worried about you."

"Why?"

"I knocked, and you didn't answer, and I listened at the door, and I didn't hear any sounds from inside."

"You're such a creeper." I glared at him, but I couldn't stop a warm feeling from growing inside of me. He had been worried. That meant he cared a little bit, at least.

"These are for you." He handed me the flowers with a small smile.

"Where did you get those at this hour?"

"The bodega down the street. I got you a bottle of wine as well. It's in my apartment still."

"Wow." I licked my suddenly dry lips. "Thank you."

"Can I come inside?" He nodded at my door, and I hesitated. I didn't know if it was smart to let him in. I was still mad at him.

"I don't have to the stay the night. I'd just like to talk."

"It's late, Carter."

"I know it's late but just for a bit. I really would like to apologize and explain."

"Fine," I said as I reached for my keys and opened the front door. "Come in."

"Hold on, let me get the wine and my guitar." He hurried toward his door and I watched as he opened it and grabbed a bottle of wine and his guitar that had been sitting there. I also saw Frosty's nose peeking out the door.

"Come on, Frosty. You can come as well," I called out to the dog, and he came running toward me with his tongue hanging out. "Hey there, boy," I said and rubbed his neck and behind his ears. "Who's a good boy?"

"Me," Carter said, and I looked up to see him standing right in front of me again.

"You're not a good boy." I gave him my sternest look and gestured him inside. "Come on, let's go inside before I change my mind."

"Come on, Frosty," he said as he pushed past me and ran into my apt. "We don't want to get locked out."

"Carter," I said in a slow drawl as I walked inside and then shut the door. "Open the wine already."

"Yes, ma'am."

"I'm going to change into my pj's," I said as I walked to my bedroom. "You can make yourself comfortable in the living room."

"Okay." He nodded, and he walked toward the kitchen. "Wait," he said as he headed back toward me and then gave me a kiss on the cheek. "I didn't greet you properly."

"Take these and put them in water," I told him as I handed him the flowers, my cheek hot from his kiss. This was all starting to feel all too comfortable and familiar, and I wasn't sure how to feel about it.

I was in the bathroom washing my face when I heard a noise behind. I turned around and saw Frosty on the ground behind me.

"Hey, sorry, I hope you don't mind." Carter walked into the bathroom behind Frosty. "We just wanted to see what you were up to."

"I was just about to put a face mask on, actually."

"Cool." He paused. "Like a mud mask? My sister always puts them on."

"No, a collagen mask. I buy them online. They're from Korea. Meant to help me keep my youthful appearance." I laughed.

"You're beautiful just as you are."

"Uh-huh," I said. "Come on." I grabbed a packet from the drawer and walked into the bedroom. "We can hang out in here."

"Can I get my guitar? I learned a new song."

"Sure," I said as I sat on the bed and undid the packet

to my mask. I peeled off the plastic and stuck the wet side onto my face.

"Oh, my word, you look like a weird ghost." Carter started laughing as he walked back into the bedroom. "Hold on a minute," he said, and I watched as he drew his phone out of his pocket and then put it up in the air.

"What are you doing?"

"I'm taking a photo of you," he said and then I heard *click*.

"Carter, no," I screeched. "That's not right."

"Why not? Now, anytime I want to see you and you're not around I can just look at this photo."

"You're horrible." I glared at him, but I wasn't sure if he could tell behind my face mask. I wanted to ask him if he thought about me a lot, but I couldn't bring myself to start such a serious conversation.

"So what's the song that you learned?" I crawled up the bed and leaned back against the headboard. "Are you comfortable, by the way," I said as I noticed that he was still wearing his black jeans and a black shirt. "Do you want to change?"

"Do you mind if I just go down to my boxers?" he asked as he started unbuttoning his shirt. I wanted to jump off of the bed and finish unbuttoning it for him, but I refused to sleep with him tonight. Not after how he'd talked to me. He wasn't out of the doghouse just because he'd given me some sunflowers. "That's fine but keep the boxers on," I said and he grinned. "Yes, ma'am." He took off his clothes quickly, and before I knew what was happening, he was sitting on the edge of the bed with his guitar in just a pair of tight white briefs. Hot!

"So, let me play the song I learned tonight," he said as he started strumming the strings. "When your legs don't work like they used to before," he sang and my jaw dropped.

"Ed Sheeran?" I gasped as he continued singing with a huge smile on his face. "You learned Ed Sheeran for me?" My heart melted as he continued to sing. He got some of the words wrong, but I didn't care. He had done this because he wanted to get on my good side again. He cared about me in his own way. I didn't know what that meant exactly, but it was a start. When he finished singing, I gestured to him to put the guitar down and come farther up the bed.

"I want you to stay tonight," I said with a small smile. "No sex, but we can make out."

"You think I'm going to stay just for a make out?" He pouted, and I slapped him in the shoulder. "Of course, I'll stay." He reached for my hand and kissed it. "It will be my honor."

"You're so smooth, aren't you," I said as he pulled me into his arms and held me to his chest. I gazed up at his face and he leaned down to peel my face mask off and then he kissed me. His lips were warm and gentle, almost teasing, and I kissed him back softly, enjoying the feel of him against my body. My hands found their way to his hair and I could feel him growing hard against me. I wanted to take his briefs off, but I stopped myself and peeled away from him.

"Too hot and heavy, big boy," I teased him as I reached down to squeeze his manhood for a few seconds. I felt pretty powerful when his body stilled, and his gaze turned to one of lust and desire. I moved my hand away and settled against his chest.

"I really am sorry about tonight," he whispered against my ear. "I believe you if you say Dante is just a friend.

Maybe I can get to know him better to overcome my dislike of him?"

"Why do you care?" I asked him softly, gazing up at him. "I thought this was just a two-night stand for you?"

"I'd like to make it a three-night stand?" His hand moved to my breast and cupped it, and I sighed. "No, but seriously," he stammered. "I don't know what I want or where this is going, but I know I have a lot of fun with you, and I enjoy being with you, and maybe we can just see . . ." His voice trailed off, and I tried not to roll my eyes. What a typical guy response. What he meant was he still wanted to have sex but didn't want a commitment.

"I don't really know what that means, Carter." I shook my head at him.

"It means I have a lot to think about right now. I'm quitting my job. I'm trying to pursue my music. I don't have time for a girlfriend." He made a face. "I can't do anything serious right now. I like you. I think you're a great girl, but I just can't be tied down right now."

"Okay," I said and looked away from him. What else could I say to that? It wasn't like he'd ever led me to believe anything different.

"Hey, look at me." His voice was husky, and I looked up into his deep soulful blue eyes. "You're special to me, Lila. I've not met a girl like you before. I want to get to know you better. I want to be the only man you fuck. I want to just take things slowly, okay?"

"Okay," I said, and I leaned up to kiss him. I felt like his words were genuine and even though they weren't the exact words I wanted to hear, they were good enough for now.

"I have another show tomorrow night. Maybe you can come?" he asked hopefully. "I can take you out to dinner beforehand?"

"You want to take me to dinner?" I feigned shock, but inside I was jumping for joy. This was a good step.

"Yes, goof," he said as he gave me a deep kiss. "Now, we better go to sleep or I'm going to have your panties off soon and we both know what would happen next."

"Night, Carter," I whispered, and we got under the covers with him spooning me from behind. His arms were wrapped around my waist and his head rested on mine. I closed my eyes and drifted off to sleep feeling warm and content as it hit me that we hadn't spent one night apart since we'd met.

"Sugar Pie Honey Bunch"

"Morning, sexy, made it to work on time?"
"Yes! :)"
"What no return compliment?"
"Like what?"
"Yes, stud."
"Hmm."
"Yes, handsome."
"Hmm."
"Yes, big boy."
"Who said it's big?"
"Lila! :p"
"I never told you it was big. :)"
"Fine. Yes, small boy, then."
"Are you crying?"
"No. I know I've got a big dick."
"Carter!"

97

"Are you asking to see a dick pic?"

"No!"

". . ."

"Do not send me a dick pic."

"I just wanted to hear you say dick."

"You didn't hear me say anything. I typed it. :p"

"Will you say it tonight?"

"At the concert?"

"No . . . later."

"Later?"

"Don't tell me no sex again tonight?"

"Carter, is that all you want me for?"

"I'm taking you to dinner tonight woman. That should answer that question."

"Dinner isn't really a date."

"Did I say it was a date?"

". . ."

"I'm joking. It's a date. You don't think it's a good date?"

"It's a bit boring."

"Then I'm taking you to a show."

"I'm coming to watch you perform. Not exactly the same thing."

"So you want a properly thought out little adventure sort of thing?"

"Yes, please."

"You're not asking much of me, are you?"

"Nope. :)"

"Let me think of something."

"Okay."

"Are you free this weekend?"

"As in tomorrow and the day after?"

"That would be this weekend."

"Maybe. Why?"

"I've got an idea for a date."

"An all-weekend date?"

"Would that be a problem?"

"No."

"Good."

"I need to get some work done if I'm going to meet you for dinner tonight. :)"

"Okay. Go work."

"Thanks, boss."

"You can call me that tonight."

I put the phone on my desk and smiled. I opened up my laptop and searched for fun date ideas. I had lied to Lila when I'd said I had an idea for a date. I had absolutely no ideas, but I did know I wanted to spend the weekend with her. I felt like I was on a natural high when I was around her. Even playing with the band felt more magical when she was in the room. There was something so infectious about her smile. She made me feel like a million dollars. When she'd gotten mad at me the night before and left the club without me I'd been so angry, and then I'd been so worried, and then Danielle had called me to tell me that I was an asshole and an idiot, and I'd known immediately that she was right.

I still thought that Dante wanted to sleep with her, but I couldn't keep pushing it if she didn't want to see it. I didn't think I was jealous though. I was just looking out for her. It was a weird situation we were in. I'd woken up this morning and just stared at her beautiful face while she slept. I'd wanted so badly to touch her and make love to her. I'd been so hard. It had been torture spending the night with her and not being inside of her. I hadn't spent the night in a woman's bed and not had sex since college. In fact, I rarely ever spent the night. I wasn't sure what had come over me.

A part of me thought she was like some sort of drug and soon I'd tire of her. I didn't want to hurt her feelings, so I didn't want to make any promises I couldn't keep. I had to admit though that I was excited to spend the evening and the weekend with her. It would be fun. It had been a long time since I'd actually wanted to spend my alone hours with a woman. Normally, I hung out with Harley or Lucas and we jammed or went for a beer. I hadn't been on a date in over a year. I'd hooked up with a couple of girls I'd met at gigs but only once or twice before dropping them. They'd all been so boring and vapid and talked about their hair and clothes. As if I cared. I didn't need a woman to talk world politics, but she had to have some sort of brain.

~

"Hey." I stood up as Lila walked into the restaurant. She walked to me with a wide smile and a light in her brown eyes. It was then that something hit me. A weird feeling in my stomach that twisted and turned and burned through the blood in my veins. I swallowed hard as she approached the table and reached forward to give me a hug.

"So sorry I'm late. I was running from the train station and then I went down the wrong street and got so lost." She giggled and gave me a wry smile. "I suck with directions."

A brief joke popped into my mind about sucking something else, but something in my brain dismissed it. That was an immature joke. I didn't want her to think I was immature.

"I'm glad you made it." I gave her a big hug, and she

gave me a quick kiss on the lips and rubbed the top of my head.

"I need a drink and lots of food. Give me all the food." She grinned. "It's good here, right?"

"The best," I said and waited for her to sit down before I sat. "What would you like to drink?"

"Red wine?" She shrugged. "That goes well with pasta, right?"

"Yeah." I nodded and called the waitress over. "I'll order some appetizers as well, okay?"

"Sure, sounds good to me."

"Was work fun today?" I inquired truly wanting to know everything about her day, her life, everything there was to know.

"It was okay." She shrugged and stifled a yawn. I looked at her face closely, and I could tell that she was tired. She'd had a long week; not helped by me and all our late nights. I bit my lower lip. Maybe it was selfish of me to be seeing her when my schedule meant I could only really see her late at night. My job as a musician would always have odd hours. There would be very few nights that I'd be able to actually see her and take her on dates. I couldn't give her any sort of normal dating situation even if I wanted to, and I was thinking that I wanted to date her. And not just as a test to see how it went. This moment felt momentous. I wasn't sure why, but I knew that Lila was someone special. It scared me slightly. I didn't want to think about it too deeply. This was going to be our fourth night in a row together. Surprisingly, that didn't scare me. What worried me more was how I felt at the thought of not spending a night with her? How had she become so important to me so quickly?

"*O*oh, I'm so full." She rubbed her stomach and groaned as we walked out of the restaurant. "I feel like I can barely walk."

"Do you want me to carry you to the bar?"

"No." She pushed me slightly as she shook her head vehemently. "There's no way I want you to try to carry me."

"Try to carry you?" I faked offense. "Do you think I don't have muscles?"

"Do you think you need muscles to carry me?" Her face looked distraught, and for a few seconds I thought I had really upset her until she started laughing. "Oh my, you should see your face, Carter. Of course, I know you have muscles. I just don't want you carrying my fat ass down Eighth Avenue after I've just stuffed my face with lasagna and bread. Oh, yeah and a Caesar salad that was one of the most delicious salads that I've ever had in my life."

"You weigh nothing." I rolled my eyes at her. That was obviously a lie, but I had learned from Danielle that you never mentioned a woman's weight. I guess that had been one perk of growing up with a sister.

"That's a lie that my doctor would not agree with." Lila laughed and linked hands with me. "Let's head to your show. Which way, Maestro?"

"This way," I said as I led her down the brightly lit streets of New York. I wanted to tell her that I was glad she wasn't stick thin. I wanted to tell her that I loved her curves, that her ass made me hard just looking at it, that I loved rubbing my hand across her stomach and down her hips, that she was all woman, but I had a feeling my words would get lost in translation. I didn't know how to tell her that I loved her body just the way it was. And I didn't want her to think that I thought that should be good enough. That my approval should make her love her body. I knew it didn't work that way, and I didn't want to give her another reason to put me on the naughty list. "So I have a little surprise for you," I said as I stopped and hailed an Uber.

"What?" Her eyes narrowed at me. "Isn't the show around here?"

"It is, but we're going somewhere else first."

"Oh, Carter." She bit down on her lower lip, and her eyes glowed. "You're such a bad boy."

"I am," I said, and I just laughed. I knew that she thought that I was taking her somewhere to fit in a quick hookup or something, but I wanted her to know that this was about more than sex for me.

"Did you get a hotel room or something?" She looked at her watch. "Because we don't have time to go back to Brooklyn and then head back here, even if we take Ubers both ways."

"Ye, of little faith," I teased her as we got into the back of the Uber. "Come here," I said as I pulled her closer to me in the back of the car. I knew that she wasn't a huge fan of public displays of affection, but I wanted to feel her next to me. "You're so sexy," I whispered in her ear. "Can you blame me for wanting you all the time?" My hand reached down to her leg and squeezed her knee. "Thanks for giving me a second chance. I know I was an idiot last night."

"It's okay," she said, and I held my breath as I felt her hand on my thigh, sliding up. "I guess this is a crazy situation," she said, and I wasn't sure if she was talking about this moment right now in the car or generally. Her hand was now at the front of my pants rubbing gently, and I stifled a groan as I could feel myself growing hard.

"Lila." I grabbed her hand and gave her a look.

"Yes, Carter?" she said innocently.

"Are you trying to drive me crazy?" I was trying to keep my voice low so as not to garner any attention from the driver. What I really wanted to do was hike up her skirt and lay her flat on the back seat or have her sit on my lap and unzip my pants. I stopped my thoughts as I was just making myself harder. "You're a bad girl, aren't you, Lila?"

"Now why would you say that?" She bit down on her lower lip and then licked her lips slowly. "I'm a good girl."

"Grr." I couldn't stop myself, and I grabbed her face and brought her toward me and gave her a deep kiss. "I want you," I whispered against her lips as the driver pulled up to our stop. "Thanks." I nodded to the grinning driver as I opened the door and waited for Lila to step out of the car.

"Um, where are we?" She looked around the street and frowned. "I don't see any hotels."

"We're not going to a hotel," I said and grabbed her hand. "Come with me." I led her into a cute small shop called, Sugar Sweet Sunshine Bakery and walked her over to the cupcake counter. "They make the best cupcakes in New York here. Better than Magnolia, better than Sprinkles, better than any cupcakes anywhere else."

"Ooh." She gasped and stared at the selection of cupcakes with an excited expression on her face that made me think of a kid seeing Santa for the first time. "You brought me to get cupcakes?"

"I know you love dessert, and I wanted you to have the best. I asked around the office and this place was recommended," I said, and I was rewarded by the happy delight in her eyes.

"Oh, Carter." She hugged me. "Thank you, this is awesome."

"You're welcome."

"I'm going to reward you tonight." She winked at me and then turned back to the cupcake display. "I don't know which one to get."

"Get as many as you want." I placed my hand on her back. "They all look delicious."

"Which one are you getting?" She looked at me briefly with a small smile.

"Oh, I don't want a cupcake for dessert." I winked at her. "There's no way they can taste as sweet as you do."

"Carter." She blushed bright red as the saleslady had chosen that exact moment to come over to serve us. "I'll have one of those, please." She pointed to a plain vanilla cupcake with a pink buttercream frosting. "And one of these." She looked at me guiltily as she pointed to a red velvet cupcake as well.

"Anything else?"

"No, no thanks," she said, and I pulled out my wallet. She shook her head to say no, and I gave her a look to silence her. "But you paid for dinner, I don't want you to pay for this as well, you're not even getting any."

"This is my treat, Lila. Tonight I'm trying to show you that I can be a gentleman sometimes." I laughed. "And part of being a gentleman and wooing a lady is to treat them."

"Carter, that sounds so old-fashioned. This isn't the fifties." She rolled her eyes at me, but I could see she was happy. And that made me happy. I didn't recognize myself as I stood there. I had never been this sickly sweet sort of guy. Never. It certainly didn't go with my rock star image. My boys wouldn't even believe it was me if they saw me now, but maybe it wouldn't be so bad. Lila wasn't pushing me for anything serious; she wasn't trying to force my hand. This was easy and fun. And we were both still able to live our normal lives. If our relationship continued like this forever, I didn't see any reason to want to stop it. The lyrics to the song, "Sugar Pie Honey Bunch" filled my mind, and a part of me wanted to sing it to her but I stopped myself. I didn't mind being sweet, but that song was way too sentimental for this moment.

~

"*A*re you guys having fun tonight?" I shouted out to the crowd. The bar was packed, and we had a sold-out show.

"Of course, they're having fun. We're fucking rocking," Harley shouted as he played the drums. "You're killing it tonight, Carter," he shouted, and I just grinned. I could see Lila sitting at a table to the right of the stage, and she was dancing, and singing along to every song with a huge smile on her face. I'd told the bartender to ensure she was never without a drink and whatever else she wanted. I wanted tonight to be perfect.

"Hey, sexy," a voice called out from the front of the stage and I looked down. It was Zola, an actress that I'd had a brief flirtation with for the last couple of months. She would come to shows and we'd banter back and forth, but I'd never actually taken her out.

"Hey." I waved down to her and watched as she put her hands up in the air and swayed back and forth as if she was a stripper. Her long black hair hung down her back, and she had striking green eyes that were giving me *come-fuck-me* vibes. I smiled at her as she did her little dance for me, her breasts almost popping out of her tight white crop top. Her olive skin glowed in the light of the bar, and I couldn't deny that she was beautiful, but I just felt nothing for her. It didn't even matter to me. I looked over to the bar and saw Lila sitting there watching me on the stage, her eyes slightly narrowed as she gazed at me and Zola. She'd noticed the little dance then, and she didn't seem happy. This made me inexplicably happy. So I wasn't the only one that didn't appreciate the other sex giving either of us unwanted attention.

"We're going to take a quick break, folks, but we'll be back in fifteen minutes," I said, and the crowd groaned as the bartender turned his R&B mix on for the interval. I headed off of the stage to go to talk to Lila, but Zola stepped in front of my path.

"Hi, Carter," she said running her hand down the front of my shirt. Her fingernails were long and red. "Good to see you." She leaned over to hug me and pushed her breasts into my chest as she stroked the side of my face, her eyelashes batting furiously as she looked at me.

"You too. How's it going?" I asked her politely.

"Great. I'm headed to Chicago next week to film a TV pilot for NBC." She grinned. "I'm super excited, but I don't want to leave New York."

"You'll be back though?"

"Yeah, but I don't know when." She pouted, and she moved closer to me. "So, I was thinking tonight would be a good night for us to finally get to know each other."

"Oh yeah?" I said and looked down at her obviously plastic breasts that were pressing into my chest.

"Yeah." She ran her hands down the sides of my arms. "I don't live far from here and . . ."

"Carter, there you are." Lila's voice interrupted Zola as she walked over to us. "I was looking for you." She gave me a tight smile and then looked at Zola. "I'm Lila, and you are?"

"Zola." Zola's voice was full of distaste. "Carter and I were just making plans for . . ."

"Come here, big boy," Lila said, and before I knew

what was happening she was pulling me toward her and kissing me in front of everyone. I didn't know what was going on, but I wasn't going to say no. I put my arms around her waist and kissed her passionately, my hand sliding down her back to her ass as she pressed herself into me. I felt her hands on my shoulders and then in my hair, and I groaned as she started sucking on my tongue. Out of the corner of my eye I could see Zola's face looking disbelieving and disgusted as she walked away, and I knew that was exactly what Lila had wanted to happen.

"I want to fuck you so badly," I groaned into Lila's ear as I pulled away slightly, feeling hard. I grabbed her hand and pulled it down to the front of my pants. "You see how hard you've got my cock."

"Let's do something about it then," she said as she squeezed it slightly and kissed me again. "Let's fuck."

"What?" My eyes widened in shock. "I'm on a fifteen-minute break. I can't leave now."

"We don't have to leave." She shook her head and grabbed my hand. "Come with me." She pulled me toward the back of the bar toward the restrooms. By luck, there happened to be a vacant restroom, and she pulled me inside with her before locking the door behind us.

"Are you sure?" I was shocked. There was no way she wanted me to fuck her in the restroom, was there? I mean, I was down for it. I'd just never thought she would be.

"Sh," she said as she pushed me back against the door and started kissing me again. Her hand reached for my zipper and pulled it down. I groaned as she freed my cock through the slit in my boxer shorts and the feel of her warm hands on me almost made me come right away. She dropped to her knees and then took me in her mouth, sucking me hard and long. I closed my eyes and rested my head against the door as her head bobbed up and down and her fingers played with my balls. I knew I was close to coming, so I pulled her away. I didn't want to come just yet. I reached for her blouse and undid the buttons and then caressed her breasts before pulling the cups of her bra down so that I could suck on her nipples. She moaned loudly as I sucked on her right nipple, and my hand moved down to pull her skirt up. I slipped her panties to the side and started rubbing her. She was already wet, and I slipped a finger inside of her. She grabbed the back of my head, and her body started squirming as I slipped another finger in and moved them back and forth quickly.

"Oh Carter," she cried out. "Please."

"Please, what?" I looked at her face that was full of desire. "What do you want, Lila?"

"I want you inside of me." She moaned. "Now."

"Yes, ma'am." I turned her around and bent her over the sink and moved my cock to her wetness and rubbed the tip against her clit for a few seconds. It was wet and ready, and I slid myself into her hungrily. She felt like heaven as I thrust into her, and as I moved back and forth she moved her hips as well, and I could feel my load building up.

"Faster," she cried out as she gripped the side of the sink. "Oh, yes, that's it," she said as I grabbed her hips and slammed into her, my cock almost falling out of her at the speed I was going. I slowed down for a few seconds and let her feel the full depth of my cock as I thrust into her with every inch of my being. She started moving her hips back and forth and slamming her ass back into me and so I increased my speed again.

"Fuck, I'm going to come." I grunted as I continued slamming into her, and it was then that I felt her orgasming on my cock, her walls tightening in on me. I reached forward to rub her clit to intensify her orgasm, and then I felt myself coming long, hard, and deep inside of her. I continued thrusting for about ten more seconds and then pulled out of her and turned her around. "That was so hot," I muttered against her lips as her eyes fluttered looking dazed and ecstatic. I kissed her hard, and then as I realized the time I pulled away. "Shit, I have to go back on stage. Is that okay?" She just nodded at me with a small smile. "We'll finish this when we get home," I said as I grabbed a tissue and wiped off my cock, and then zipped my pants back up.

"I can't wait." She grinned, and I leaned forward to kiss her again before exiting the restroom and going back on the stage, feeling higher than I had in years.

LILA

"I'll Make Love To You"

"Fuck, fuck, fuck," I said as I paced around my bathroom. It had been three weeks since Carter and I had unprotected sex in the bar, and now my period was late. I bit down on my lower lip and looked at my calendar again. I was only three days late. It's just a few days. I knew that could be a possibility even though I'd always been on schedule before. "Shit," I said as I sat down on the toilet seat. I couldn't believe that I'd been so irresponsible. I knew it took two to tango, and Carter hadn't seemed concerned about birth control either, but I had a feeling that maybe he had assumed I was on the pill or something. He'd never asked me about what contraception I used and we'd always used a condom before and after that.

Everything the last three weeks had been pretty amazing. In fact, it had been the best three weeks I could remember having ever. We'd spent every night together, and even though we hadn't always hung out if I had to work late or he had a show, we'd texted throughout the day so I always felt like I knew what he was up to. Danielle was coming back in two days, and he was going to be moving back to his place in Manhattan. I wasn't sure what that would mean for our nightly sleepovers, but I was confident we would still see each other. We weren't technically in a relationship as Carter still seemed loathe to make any real sort of commitment. I'd asked if he wanted to take a trip to Hawaii at some point, and he'd kinda changed the subject, but I had understood. He had given his notice at work and this was his last week before he transitioned to becoming a full-time musician. "Fuck," I said again as I sat there. If I was pregnant, everything would become so much more complicated. I didn't even know how I would tell him. What would he say? How would he react?

"What you doing?" My phone beeped, and I saw that it was Carter texting. Normally, I was happy to see a text from him, but now he was the last person I wanted to talk to. I looked at the text and decided not to reply. I didn't want to see him right now. We hadn't made plans for the day because he wasn't sure if he had practice with Harley and I was glad for it. I needed to go to Walgreens and grab a pregnancy test or two and figure out what was going on. I jumped up and walked into the bedroom and grabbed my handbag so that I could head to the store. I didn't want to just sit around and wait for the answer. I needed to know now.

"Hey, you around?" My phone beeped with another message, and I shoved my phone in my handbag after putting it on silent. I didn't want to deal with him right now. I hurried to my front door and opened it slowly and walked on tippy toes out to the hallway and then closed it

as quietly as possible. I walked to the staircase quickly, and then once there I ran down the steps and exited the building. I did not want to see Carter on my way to Walgreens. I didn't need him tagging along and asking me what I wanted to buy. Once in Walgreens, I hurried to the pregnancy test section and picked up four different boxes. Four different boxes couldn't all be wrong, I thought to myself and then hurried to the cashier. I could see my phone blinking as I grabbed my wallet, but I ignored it. I hurried back to my apartment and ran up the stairs. I'd had a lot of water to drink that morning, and it was all ready to come out, which was great news for my pregnancy tests. I was feeling pleased with myself until I got to the top of the stairs.

"Oh," I said as I saw Carter standing there with Frosty on a leash. "Hi." I offered him a weak smile.

"Hi." He gave me a suspicious look. "Where have you been? I've been texting you all morning."

"Oh, just running some errands," I said with a bright smile and tried to hide the Walgreens bag behind my back.

"What errands?" His eyes narrowed.

"This and that."

"This and that, huh?" He walked toward me. "Is there something you're not telling me, Lila?"

"What?" I said slowly. "What do you mean?"

"What's in the bag you're hiding behind your back?" he asked with a raised eyebrow.

"Nothing." I could feel my face going red.

"Lila."

"It's nothing," I said and looked down. Why was he pushing this? "Don't you need to walk Frosty?"

"We just got back," he said as he shook his head, and then before I knew what was happening he had grabbed the bag from my hand and was opening it up. "What's this?" He frowned as he pulled one of the pink boxes out. "First Response?" He read out loud, and I wanted to die. "First Response?" His eyes flew to mine and then back to the box. "First Response Pregnancy. Only brand that can tell you six days sooner than your missed period," he read and then looked me in the eyes again. "What is this?" His blue eyes looked confused for a few seconds, and then something must have dawned on him because his face turned to one of shock and surprise. "Are you pregnant?" He blinked as if the words were foreign to him.

"I don't know. That's why I'm taking the test." I grabbed the box and the bag back from him. "Excuse me, please."

"You weren't going to tell me?" He followed me to my front door.

"Tell you what? I don't even know if I'm pregnant yet. I just know my period is late."

"You sure it's mine?" he said behind me, and I turned around and gasped at him. He had a wry smile on his face as he put his hands up. "Poor joke, I'm sorry."

"That's not even funny, Carter." I opened the door and walked into the apartment. "Really poor taste."

"I know, I know." He followed me in and undid Frosty's leash as he closed the door behind me. "I would ask how this happened, but I do remember a certain night where we . . ."

"I don't need you to fill me in, Carter, I was there." I rolled my eyes at him. "I'm going to go and take the test now," I said as I headed toward my bedroom. "You can come if you want, but not into the bathroom," I stammered to add. "Just sit in the bedroom."

"Okay." He nodded as he followed me. "I'd been meaning to ask you if you were on the pill or had an IUD or something . . ." His voice trailed off. "I guess the answer is no."

"The answer is no." I walked into the bathroom and closed the door behind me. "Idiot," I whispered under my breath.

"I heard that." He laughed from the other side of the door and then I heard him singing a Boyz II Men song. "I'll make love to you, like you want me to."

"Are you standing right outside?" I asked as I opened the box and took the plastic device out of its foil and hurried to the toilet to pee on it. I really didn't need to hear his cheerful singing right now. I knew he had to be freaking out inside.

"Yes," he said, his voice loud. "I wouldn't mind coming in."

"Nope," I shouted and then closed my eyes to pretend he wasn't there. I peed onto the stick, placed it on the counter, and then flushed the toilet. I opened the door to see Carter standing there with anticipation in his eyes and Frosty spread out on my bed.

"So?" he asked his eyes wide. "Are you pregnant?"

"Carter, I have to wait five minutes before I will know." I walked over to the bed and stroked the top of Frosty's head. "And I don't even know how accurate these things are."

"That's why you got four?" he asked and came and sat down next to me. He was acting surprisingly calm given the situation.

"Yeah." I nodded and stared into his eyes. He leaned forward and kissed me on the lips.

"It'll be okay, you'll see."

"You think so?" I asked him.

"Yeah, it's very unlikely you're pregnant, right? I mean we only had unprotected sex that one time and it was a quickie." He paused. "I sound stupid right now, don't I? Like some sort of dumb teenager."

"You put the words right into my mouth." I laughed at him. "It doesn't matter if it was a quickie," I said. "You can get pregnant rather fast. Those sperm can swim, you know."

"Yeah." He nodded. "And I'm sure my bad boys are like champion swimmers as well," he said proudly, and I hit him in the shoulder.

"You really are a fool, Carter Stevens."

"Sh," he said and looked toward the bathroom door. "Is it time for you to check yet?"

"Hmm, I guess," I said and stood up, my heart racing. He stood up behind me, and we walked to the bathroom together. "So one line is not pregnant and two lines is pregnant," I told him as we walked into the bathroom. "You look, I'm scared to."

"Okay." He nodded and picked up the stick. He looked at it for a few seconds before speaking, and I couldn't tell what he was thinking. "So one line is not pregnant, right?"

"Yes, thank God." I ran over to him and kissed him on the lips. "Phew, that was a close call."

"Um," He looked down at me, his blue eyes dancing. "Two lines means pregnant though, right?"

"Yes, why?"

"Because there are two lines, Lila," he said, his voice in awe and his eyes wide. "We're having a baby."

"Twinkle Twinkle, Little Star"

My muscles felt taut as I ran, but I didn't stop. In fact, I started running faster, trying to catch up with the cyclists that had just past me. *Concentrate on the running, Carter, concentrate on the running.* My mind didn't want to concentrate on the running, it wanted to think about the fact that I was going to be a dad. How was this possible? My heart thudded as I ran even faster, and it wasn't due to the adrenaline of pushing myself from running the entire circumference of Prospect Park.

Was the sex worth it? A demon in my head said. *This is what you get for thinking with your dick.* I looked at a mother pushing a stroller on the pavement to the right of me and there was a massive smile on her face. I could see her diamond ring sparkling in the sunlight and I wondered if Lila had gotten pregnant to try to trap me into marrying her. Immediately I felt ashamed of myself for the thought.

Lila wasn't that sort of girl and if I was honest, she'd looked even more terrified than I had when I'd said she was pregnant. Granted, we weren't one hundred percent sure, she was going to the doctors to check. She was most probably there right now, in fact.

Fuck. My calves were cramping up, but still I persisted. I'd been running for ten miles already. I hadn't run over five miles since my high school track days, and my body was going to hate me tomorrow for pushing it so hard today. I didn't care. I would most probably have more worries than aching muscles to think about tomorrow. What was I going to do with a baby? I didn't even like babies. They cried. They pooped. They looked weird. And how was this going to work with Lila? I had no doubt in my mind she would make a great mother. She was a wonderful caring human being, after all, but that didn't mean it was right for us to have a baby together. And I wasn't sure what kind of dad I would make. I heard my phone ringing then, and I didn't check it. I didn't want to look and see that it was Lila. I didn't want the reality of the situation to come to fruition. How was I going to tell Danielle? She went away for a month, and I looked after her dog who looked to me as if he had gained weight, and I'd gotten her friend and neighbor pregnant.

"Welcome back, sis, you're going to be an aunt." I groaned as I ran, and then I tripped on a small pebble and nearly went crashing into the ground. I stopped running and took a deep breath. I walked over to the grass and lay down and looked up at the sky. It was a bright sunny day, and the sky was a beautiful light blue with big fluffy white clouds. I played with the grass as I lay there and then took a few deep breaths. For some reason, the lyrics to "Twinkle Twinkle Little Star" started running through my mind. I'd have to go from singing rock to singing nursery rhymes. I groaned again. This was why I didn't see women more than once a week and this was why I didn't date. I just hooked up. Because when you date you get comfortable. And when you date you make stupid mistakes. When you date you get the girl you've been sleeping with for a month or so pregnant. Granted, this most probably wasn't the norm, and I should have had my head screwed on straight at all times, but it was too late to blame myself now.

My phone was ringing again, and I sighed as I pulled it out of my pocket. Guess it was time to adult and face the music.

"Hey, so boy or girl?"

"What?" Harley's voice drawled into the phone. "What are you talking about? Are you dating dudes now?"

"Harley, shut up." I wasn't in the mood for his crap. "What do you want?"

"Way to treat your best friend and bandmate."

"You're not my best friend. What's up?"

"Yo, dude, chill, what's up?" He sounded concerned.

"It's a long story." I sighed. "Let's just say I might be a dad soon."

"Thought that would have happened sooner."

"Really, dude? Like really?" I was getting annoyed.

"Who's the unlucky mama?"

"The blonde you saw at the show."

"Oh, big tits?"

"Harley, I swear . . ." I growled.

"My bad, she's your baby mama now." He laughed, and I clenched my fist.

"What the fuck do you want, dude?" I was about to hang up on him.

"So, the execs from Universal called me, they tried to call you, but you didn't answer. Anyway, they got a gig for us in Canada to test the market and see how people like us."

"Canada?" I said, jumping up. "When?"

"In a couple of months."

"Okay." I nodded. "That's doable. For how long?"

"Two weeks. And, dude, the pay is good. Twenty grand for you and me, and ten grand for Lucas."

"Not bad." I grinned into the phone, suddenly feeling better. This was awesome. We were finally getting a break.

"I think we need to call Carlos, dude, we need a manager now, and he's a manager and a lawyer so he can really help us out with contracts and stuff."

"Yeah, yeah," I agreed. Carlos was Harley's pool buddy from the Bronx and he knew the business inside out. We hadn't hired him before because we'd only played local gigs, but now this was getting serious, we needed someone who knew what he was doing. "Try and get him to take five percent. I don't want to be giving away ten percent."

"Yeah, I'll talk to him, man," Harley drawled, and then he spoke in a serious voice. "So what are you going to do about the baby? You guys keeping it?"

"What do you mean?" I frowned into the phone.

"Are you guys keeping it, you know?" His voice was lower. "I mean, there are options, man, if you're not ready."

"We're keeping it," I said immediately as a little baby with Lila's smiling brown eyes flashed into my mind. There was no doubt in my mind that if she was pregnant, we were keeping it. Unless of course, she didn't want to. What if she didn't want to? My heart started racing fast. What would I do? What would I say? I didn't even know if I had the option to say anything? Did my opinion matter? And did I even have a right to an opinion if I was avoiding her calls? "Look I got to go," I said suddenly. I had to call Lila.

I had to find out if she was definitely pregnant or not. And what she wanted to do. I hung up without waiting for Harley to speak and looked at my missed calls. None of them were actually from Lila. She hadn't called me after all, and I felt angry. Why hadn't she called me to update me? I checked my texts, and there was nothing from her there either.

"Hey, what's going on?" I texted her. I had a feeling that if I called I might sound angry, and I didn't want to sound angry.

"Just sitting here waiting." She texted me back immediately and I let out a sigh of relief. Okay, so she hadn't been withholding the news on me.

"If you're pregnant, we're having the baby, right?" I texted, knowing that this was not an appropriate conversation to have via text message but not being able to stop myself.

"Huh?"

"We're going to have the baby if you're pregnant, right?"

"Hold on, nurse just came in . . ."

I stared at the screen my heart racing.

"What did she say?" I waited with bated breath for the answer. What if she wasn't pregnant after all? What if there was no baby after all this? I felt a sudden disappointment as the image of the small baby with Lila's brown eyes and cute smile popped into my face. We'd have a beautiful baby if she was pregnant.

"I'm pregnant." She typed about five minutes later, and the relief I felt shocked me. *"Are you okay?"* She typed again when I hadn't responded.

"Yes." I typed back. *"Can I come over?"*

"I'll be home in an hour."

"Great. I'll see you then."

∿

"*H*ey," Lila said as she opened her front door. She was wearing a pair of blue jeans and a Hawkeyes sweater. Her hair was up in a messy ponytail, and her face was clean of makeup. She looked beautiful and sweet, and I just wanted to pull her into my arms.

"Hey," I said. "I got this for you." I held up a little stuffed elephant toy that I'd bought in a store on my way back from the park and handed it to her. "For the baby."

"What?" She looked at me like I was crazy and then started laughing. "Oh, Carter."

"What?" I said. "Babies love teddy bears right? I loved them when I was a kid."

"There's a lot more for us to think about than that." She shook her head as she gazed at me with a tender expression in her eyes. "You should come in."

"Thanks," I said as I followed her in, and we headed toward the living room.

"Want a drink?" she offered, and I shook my head.

"How are you feeling?" I asked her as we sat down on the couch. "Do you need anything?"

"Carter, I literally just found out I'm pregnant." She touched my arm. "I'm fine. I don't need anything."

"Okay." I nodded. "Makes sense. So . . ." I started to talk, but all of a sudden words failed me. What the hell did I say now?

"Yes?"

"I'm not ready to get married," I blurted out. "I mean I know people get married for kids all the time, and I think that's noble, but I don't think we should rush into anything too serious." I groaned as I listened to the words I'd just said. "Sorry, that came out wrong."

"Carter, I'm not expecting you to marry me." She

looked down at her lap. "Don't worry about it. Actually, I have something to tell you."

"Oh?" Oh my God, was she going to tell me that Dante was the father? If she told me that, I swore I would lose it. After all her denials. I would lose it. My eyes narrowed as I looked at her and then at her stomach. I looked back up at her face, and she had a small smile as she stared at me.

"What are you thinking right now, Carter?"

"You don't want to know."

"I'm sure I already know." She sighed. "You're really an idiot, you know that, right?"

"I'm the idiot? What?"

"Look, Carter, I'm going to Iowa tomorrow."

"What?" My jaw dropped, and I could feel myself growing nervous. "Forever?"

"No." She shook her head. "For a couple of weeks. I have some vacation time, and I haven't seen my parents in ages. I need to just go home and think for a bit."

"You mean away from me?"

"No, I just mean away from the city and work and everything." She shrugged. "This is life-changing news for me. I need to figure out how I'm going to handle it."

"What do you mean?" My heart froze.

"I mean, I'm keeping the baby, but I'm not sure if the city is a great place to be a single mom." She sighed. "I don't know how I'm going to do this."

"I'm still here," I said with a frown. "I'll be able to help." But I wasn't really sure how true that was or how feasible. Wasn't I just about to go to Canada for two weeks, and what if the band really picked up and got world tours? What help would I be then?

"Really?" She looked doubtful. "I mean you just quit

your job to become a musician. I'm not sure how much time you'll have."

I started to feel guilty and annoyed at the same time. This was my dream. This had always been my dream. Granted I was thirty now and should be responsible, but I didn't want this. I didn't want to be settled down with a kid. This wasn't the life I had signed up for. I was starting to feel like I was going to be trapped into a life I didn't really want.

"Carter, look at me," she snapped, and I looked into her eyes. "Your face looks absolutely miserable." She sighed. "Look, I'm not asking you to be a part of this baby's life. I know you weren't even looking for a serious relationship, so a baby was not part of your equation. I'm an adult. I can look after this baby by myself. You don't even have to pay child support. I know you won't have any income once you quit your job."

"You make me sound like a deadbeat dad." I was angry again. "I will pay for my child, Lila."

"I don't think you will be a deadbeat dad." Her voice was soft, and she took a hold of my hands. "I just don't want you to feel any pressure. I know your career as a musician is important to you. I know that you've been waiting for this moment for your whole life. I want you to go out and pursue your dreams, Carter." Her voice was so caring that it immediately made me feel guilty. How could she be so thoughtful to me in this situation? I was an insensitive jerk. I knew it at that moment as surely as I knew that I had blond hair and blue eyes. I was an asshole, and if Danielle found herself in a situation with a guy like me, I would beat him up.

"I don't deserve you." I sighed as I moved her fingers up and kissed them. "We'll figure this out, I promise."

"I know we will." She smiled. "This is a good thing. Or it will be."

"God, I hated picking up Frosty's poop. I can't imagine cleaning a baby's dirty butt." I made a face, and she laughed, her eyes crinkling as she threw her head back. She grabbed a hold of my face and kissed me, her hands running through my hair, and I kissed her back eagerly, loving how her lips against mine just felt so right. We fell back onto the couch, and I ran my hands down her arms and cupped her breasts.

"I guess we can't do it anymore, huh?" I muttered regretfully as I felt myself growing hard against her.

"Huh?" She looked confused.

"Now that you're pregnant?"

"Oh, you goof, of course, we can." She laughed, and I watched as she pulled her sweater off and threw it on the ground. "Get your clothes off, Carter." She winked at me and wiggled on the couch as she started taking her jeans off. I reached for my T-shirt and started pulling it off, and as I gazed at her giggling on the couch it suddenly hit me that I loved this woman, and it was at that moment that I started to feel even more scared.

"*I* Don't Love You Much Do I?"

Beep beep. My phone made the familiar noise that alerted me to the fact that I had a text message. I smiled when I saw Carter's name on the screen. Maybe he missed me like I was missing him. We'd been texting back and forth every day but hadn't really said much asides from checking up on each other's days. I'd been in Iowa for a week now, and my parents were driving me crazy. They had been shocked to hear that I was pregnant and not engaged and had been spending the last couple of days trying to convince me why I should just stay in Iowa and not even go back to New York; even trying to say that my Uncle Robert could drive to the city in his truck and pick up my stuff to bring back to Des Moines. I was ready to leave, but I still needed to figure out what do without Carter right there in my head. Not that he wasn't in my head still, but at least he wasn't there in my bed every night. The lines had become so blurred between us that I wasn't even sure what to think or feel anymore. I unlocked my phone screen to see what Carter had to say.

"Hey, where are you?"

"I'm at the park. Why?"

"I saw your post on Instagram."

"Yeah and?"

"It was of your dog with his head out of the window and I was wondering how you took the photo if you were driving?" I could feel my face starting to heat up. Was he about to tell me off again? I couldn't believe how bossy and controlling he was, mostly because he hadn't been that way at all when we'd first met. He'd been so carefree and light as if nothing could ever bother him. Now I felt like he was my dad. In fact, he was worse than my dad had ever been. It seemed he was always on my ass about something.

"Yeah, it was my parents, dog, Dumbo? I took him to the park."

"Did you take the photo while at a light?"

"Sorry, what?"

"The photo looked like the car was moving."

"Huh?"

"Don't drive and text."

"I wasn't texting."

"Don't drive and take photos."

"Okay." I rolled my eyes at his text. I hadn't actually been moving when I'd taken the photo as I'd been at a red light.

"You have to be responsible now, Lila."

"I have to be responsible?" My jaw dropped as I read his text message. Was he for real? *Mr. I gave up my job to make it as a musician?* Granted he hadn't known he was going to be a father at that point and really it wasn't like I wanted him to have to work a job he hated just because we hadn't prac- ticed safe sex, but he made like no money now. Not that I

needed his money, but still. Ugh, it was all so frustrating and aggravating.

"When are you back?"

"Next week."

"Good."

"Good?"

"There are some things we need to discuss."

"Oh?"

"I think we should move in together while we try to figure out what's best for the baby."

"Live together? The baby isn't even here yet."

"I think it's for the best."

"Carter . . ." I didn't even know what else to say. Had he lost his mind? He wanted us to live together. I felt a little thrill at the thought, but it wasn't practical for us to live together or smart. Hadn't he said he didn't want to get married just because we were having a baby? How was living together much better?

"I'll pick you up at the airport and we can discuss further. Send me your flight info."

"I don't need you to pick me up."

"Send it to me, Lila or I will come to Iowa and pick you up there. Talk soon."

And with that. I knew he wasn't going to be responding to any more of my texts that day even though he was the one that had initiated the whole conversation. Carter had a way of backing off and ignoring me when he was mad at me or didn't get his way. It was one of his most annoying habits, and I didn't really understand why he thought it was okay to just ignore me when he was frustrated with me. It was like he was trying to punish me for my behavior because he knew how much I hated being ignored. I'd have to speak to him about it when I got back. I hadn't wanted to in the beginning because, well; I hadn't wanted to be one of those women that was all demanding and complaining; especially when we hadn't even been in a real relationship, but now it was getting ridiculous. And while we still technically weren't in a relationship, I didn't know what we were. We were about to have a child together, and we needed to have much more open communication and not just in the bedroom. In the bedroom, we had no problems at all. In the bedroom we were dynamite. It was weird how neither one of us had any reservations in the bedroom; especially me. I'd never been able to tell a man what I wanted him to do so easily and so casually before. Maybe it was because I wasn't trying to impress Carter in the bedroom, or maybe it was because I'd gone into this knowing it was going to be a fling. Whatever it was we'd gelled immediately. Our bodies were almost made for each other. It was like we were out of our own heads when we made love. We were so caught up in the ecstasy of the moment that nothing else really mattered. But then again that ecstasy had gotten us into the place we were now.

"He is so bossy and arrogant. He thinks he can just tell me what to do," I mumbled to myself as I looked around for Dumbo. "Come on, Dumbo, we have to go home." Dumbo looked at me from about five yards away and then ran in the opposite direction to go and play with some other dogs. Typical Dumbo, I thought. He loved the dog park, and it was always a hassle getting him to leave. He reminded me a little bit of Carter in that they were both stubborn and set in their ways. It made me worry that our baby would be like that; totally wanting his or her own way all the time. Oh God, I didn't know what I would do if our baby turned out to be as stubborn and boorish as Carter. I didn't know how I'd cope. For a few seconds, I thought about a little baby boy or girl giving me the obstinate look that Carter sometimes did and I groaned, and then something in me started to warm. Our baby would be cute, even with the obstinate face. I hoped our baby would have his big blue eyes. I loved Carter's eyes. There was something so dreamy and teasing about them. And even though I'd always thought blue eyes could be so cold at times, his eyes were always warm and welcoming. I always felt at home when I looked into Carter's eyes. I always felt at ease.

He was so dreamy when he wasn't being an arrogant bossy boots. My heart melted when I thought about us having a baby together and him holding her. He'd make a good dad, I thought. He was loving and caring and protective, and he would love our baby. I knew that without a doubt. He'd already bought the baby a toy. That made me laugh.

I knew he was scared because I was scared as well, but I knew in my heart that he would make the best dad. I cradled my stomach for a few seconds, feeling slightly stupid, because I wasn't showing at all and my baby was likely the size of a peanut or something right now, but there was a life growing inside of me and it made me happy. I realized then that I was happy to be having this baby. I could do this. No matter what happened with Carter, I could do this. And it was at that moment that I knew that I wanted more. I wanted us to be a family. I was in love with Carter Stevens, flaws and all, and that scared me because I had no idea what was going to happen. We barely knew each other, but we were going to have a baby. I knew that I would move in with him. It would be a test to see if we could be together. It would be a test to see if he could fall in love with me as well.

"I don't love you much do I, just more than human tongue can tell that's all," I sang a Guy Clarke song that my grandad had always sung to my grandmother. It had always made me feel weepy because he had loved her so much. That was what I wanted for Carter and me. That was what I wanted for our baby. I wanted us to be a happy family. I wanted us to be deeply in love. I wanted him to not be able to imagine his life without me. I wanted the picture-perfect family, and I wanted it with him. I smiled to myself as I thought about the hot sex that we had. I wanted that to remain as well. I wanted us to still keep our adventurous side. I wanted to explore my wild side with him. I laughed to myself as I realized that I was totally losing my mind.

"Dumbo, come on, we have to go," I shouted to the dog that was staring at me from across the park. He knew I wanted to leave, and he knew he was in trouble for not listening to me, but he still didn't care. I ran across the park to catch up to him. "Dumbo, come on," I shouted as I reached him, and then he started dodging and darting as he ran toward me and away again, his tongue hanging out, happy at the game he thought we were playing. "Dumbo, you have five seconds." I stopped still and raised my voice. Finally, he came running up to me with his tail wagging. I quickly released him and gave him a treat. "Come on, boy. It's time to go home," I said as I headed toward my car with a smile on my face. I put him in the back seat and then checked my phone quickly before I turned the ignition.

"Didn't mean to be bossy. I miss you. Text me your flight details, please. Have a great time in Iowa, and I can't wait to see you." I smiled at the text from Carter. Oh, how I was falling for this man. I was about to put the phone back in my bag when another text came through.

"Can't wait to kiss you and make love to you again. It feels weird sleeping without you. :P" The last text made my heart melt. Maybe there was hope after all. If he missed me, it had to mean something.

"*Y*ou Can Find Me in The Club"

"*D*on't mess this up, big brother," Danielle lectured me as I walked into the airport. "I absolutely cannot believe you guys are pregnant."

"It's not like we planned it."

"Yeah, I don't think that this would be anything any two people would plan after having known each other a little over a month."

I didn't bother to correct her and tell her we hadn't even known each other a month before we got pregnant. I mean, we had known each other over a month when we'd found out, but we'd gotten pregnant earlier than that. I almost couldn't believe it myself. It was quite possibly the most irresponsible I'd ever been.

"Are you listening to me, Carter?" Danielle started lecturing me and I wanted to tell her that it was her bossiness that most probably was making her fail in the relationship department. It was a bit like the pot calling the kettle black and I also didn't want her to be mad with me. I needed her in my court right now.

"I'm listening. Look I'm walking into La Guardia now. We'll see you when we get back, okay?"

"Okay," she said sounding amused. "Who would have thought my big brother would finally be growing up?"

"Whatever," I said, but I couldn't stop myself from laughing. "You're a brat."

"Whatever, doofus. Give Lila my love and see you guys soon," she said and then hung up. I smiled at the phone and then looked to see if I had any texts. I didn't want Lila to think that I wasn't coming if she'd texted me or something, but there were no missed texts.

I walked toward the arrival gates feeling excited. I hadn't seen Lila in a little over two weeks, and I missed her more than I'd thought would be possible in such a short time frame. She had been in my dreams and in my mind most of my waking moments and even performing shows hadn't felt the same without her there. It wasn't just because she wasn't there; it was because I knew she also wouldn't be home waiting for me when my night was over. It had been nice having someone to go back to at the end of a gig. Especially, someone like Lila that was so supportive and sexy.

I stood waiting at the arrival gate anxiously. I didn't know where her mind was at. We hadn't spoken in the last week at all. She'd asked me to not contact her after she'd sent her flight information. She said she had needed some time to think about things, and that was difficult with me being in contact with her. I didn't understand or like it and had started to contact her several times, but I'd stopped myself. I wanted to respect her wishes, and I also felt that maybe she'd been smart to say that we should have a little bit of distance.

People started to walk out of the gate, and I put my phone in my back pocket. I held up the sign I'd made on a white piece of cardboard. It read, "I met you, and you met me, little did we know, we'd create a baby." I knew it was corny, but I wanted her to laugh when she saw me. I wanted her to seriously consider living with me. I knew it was a big step, and I knew that it was something that ruined better relationships than ours, but I figured it would be the best way to really get to know each other and figure out what we were going to do once the baby came.

"Carter." Lila walked toward me rolling her red suitcase and smiled. She looked at the sign and laughed as she stopped in front of me. I put the sign down and gave her a huge hug, holding her tight to me.

"Hey you," I said and kissed her cheek.

"Hey you," she said and laughed again rubbing the side of my face. "I like the facial hair," she said as she ran her fingers along my newly grown beard. "Sexy."

"I'm glad you think so." I took the suitcase from her and walked toward the exit. "Let's just get a yellow cab home. We would have to go to another terminal for the Uber and that's just too much bother."

"We don't have to do that." She shook her head. "We can take public transportation. It's much cheaper."

"We're not taking buses and trains home." I frowned. "It's too much, and I'd rather we take a cab."

"Fine," she said, and she just looked ahead.

"What?" She looked like she was annoyed with me, and I had no idea why.

"We shouldn't be wasting money. And I don't want you wasting your money getting cabs when you don't even have a job anymore."

"I'm not a broke-ass, Lila. I have savings, and I've already got a new gig signed up," I said as I stopped to look at her seriously. "You don't have to worry about me having enough money."

"What's the gig?" she asked, looking at me curiously. I hadn't wanted to tell her just yet, but I guess there was no time like the present.

"Harley knows this manager guy Carlos, and he talked to the guys at Universal and they've offered us a two-month gig to play shows in Canada and parts of the States. They're going to pay us forty thousand dollars each."

"Whoa, what?" Her eyes widened, but I couldn't tell what she was thinking. "Wow, that's amazing. What parts of the States?"

"Mainly in the South and the Midwest. They have the best test markets for new rock bands, supposedly," I said. "We wouldn't have any shows in New York."

"Oh."

"We'd be leaving in a month."

"Oh." She licked her lips, and her eyes looked away from mine. I wanted to ask her what she was thinking and feeling. I wanted to know if she was happy for me, but I didn't know what to say. I didn't know if she thought I was deserting her.

"It's a really good opportunity. If it goes well, we could book gigs in Europe as an opening act for some big bands, maybe even The Rolling Stones."

"Europe, huh?" She looked back at me and smiled. "That's really awesome. Congrats."

"Obviously, this would complicate things a bit." I sighed. I wanted to ask her if she would tour with me, but I didn't even know if that would be feasible. She had a job, and she was pregnant. Why would she come with me? Especially because I still didn't know what I wanted.

"No, why would it?" she said. Her voice sounded higher than normal, and I stopped to stare at her properly. Her eyes were wide, and she looked like she was about to cry. My heart stopped for a moment, and I wondered what was wrong.

"Are you okay?" I asked her softly, my heart thudding. She didn't look like she was happy. Maybe she had decided in the week that we hadn't seen each other that she no longer wanted to be with me. "What's wrong?"

"Nothing's wrong." She shook her head. "Nothing at all. So when do you go?"

"We haven't signed the contract yet? We're still waiting on a few things to be ironed out. It might not even go through," I said grabbing her hand. "The music business is crazy. One day you're hot, and one day you're not."

"You guys will never be not hot," she said, her voice soft. "You're all very talented."

"Thanks, Lila," I said as we waited in line for the yellow taxi. "So have you given any thought to us living together?" I asked. "I've been thinking about it, and I've come up with a plan."

"Let's talk about it later," she said, giving me a kiss on the cheek. "I think we have a lot to talk about."

~

"We're going out tonight, Lila. You and me. We're going to dance and have fun and catch up." Danielle hugged Lila close as she walked into the apartment. "I've missed you."

"I've missed you too." Lila laughed, and we all headed back to the living room. "You have to tell me all about London, and the job, and that guy you sent me the photo of. What happened with him?"

"Oh my God, he was a loser. You will not believe what happened." Danielle groaned. "I thought he was going to be this charming English polite gentleman, but no he was this weird-ass guy with a foot fetish, and he wanted me to dress up in diapers."

"No way." Lila burst out laughing. "Baby diapers?"

"Nooo," Danielle squealed. "The adult ones for when you can't hold it in anymore."

"I think it's called incontinence, Lila," I said as I watched the two of them gossiping. "And as your brother, I want to officially state that I have no interest in hearing about this conversation."

"Sh, Carter," Lila and Danielle said in unison and both of them started laughing. They looked at me, and I glared at them, and that got them to giggling. Women! It then struck me that if Lila and I had a girl, I would be surrounded by estrogen. That couldn't happen. I would die. I really, really hoped we were having a boy.

"Are we having a boy or a girl?" I blurted out looking at Lila, and she just grinned at me.

"Brother dearest, it's too early to know the gender of the baby." Danielle just rolled her eyes at me. "He's so worried that he's going to be surrounded by women," she said to Lila. "Poor baby."

"Shut up, Danielle." I made a face at her, but then we both laughed. It felt good to be back in Lila's apartment and having a good time. It seemed like all of our conversations recently had been so serious, and it felt nice to just have a laugh. "And Lila can't go out with you tonight, she's staying in with me."

"I don't think so, big brother." Danielle grinned. "I already texted Lila yesterday, and we made plans for tonight." She looked at her watch then. "Okay, our dinner reservation is in an hour. I'm going to go and shower and start getting ready."

"Oh, yes, I should shower and get ready as well." Lila gave me a sheepish grin. "You can stay here if you want."

"And look after Frosty." Danielle laughed. "It will be good babysitting practice for you."

"I already looked after your damn dog for a month by myself," I said feeling irritated. I wanted to spend the night with Lila. I'd had visions of us going out for a romantic dinner and then coming home and making love. In fact, I was annoyed that Danielle had wanted to even come over tonight period. I'd wanted to rip Lila's clothes off as soon as we walked through the door. Having to just sit there and keep my hands to myself and wait for my sister to show up had been torture.

"Well, you've got another night of it tonight, Daddy dearest." Danielle started laughing. "Okay, I'm going to head out. Come with me, Carter, I'll grab Frosty, and you can walk him while I get ready."

"Wow, is this what my life has come to?" I threw my hands up in the air and just fake-glared at the two women that were totally dictating my life right now. "No one would believe that I was a rock star." I walked over to Lila and gave her a huge kiss before following Danielle to the front door. "Okay, I'll be back in about thirty minutes," I said and blew Lila a kiss as I exited. It felt nice to be here with her, and even though I was upset she was going out, I was happy just to be in her space again. My phone beeped as I closed the door, and I pulled it out to see a message from Harley. *"Call me now."* It read and I sighed and pressed his number into the phone.

"What's up?" I asked as he answered the phone on the first ring.

"Dude, you haven't sent the contract back. Carlos told me that you said you needed to think about it."

"I've got a lot going on right now, Harley."

"This doesn't have to do with big tits again, does it?"

"Dude, if you call her that again. I will knock your teeth out."

"What's the fucking hold up, man? The terms of the contract are exactly what we asked for. They are giving us everything we want. They want us badly, dude. We're so hot right now, we're going to burn."

"This might not be the best time for me." I kept my voice low. I didn't want Danielle to hear my conversation. I didn't want her telling Lila what she'd heard. Not after I'd told Lila I hadn't received the contract as yet. I didn't want the questions or the guilt she might feel if I decided not to go. I didn't know what I was going to do yet. I wanted to go, of course, I wanted to go. Music was my life. It had always been my life. This was my dream. We were on the precipice of fame and glory. We were about to make it. Unfortunately, I didn't know if that was everything I wanted anymore.

"What the fuck, Carter, don't let some pussy fuck this up for us." Harley was angry as he shouted in the phone, and I knew he had a right to be angry, but I didn't appreciate how he talked about Lila. I didn't appreciate it at all.

"I have to go. I'll call you tomorrow," I said and then hung up the phone. Everything in my life was upside right now, and I didn't know if I was coming or going, and I didn't want anyone to pressure me into making a decision I didn't want to make. I realized that this was the first time in my thirty years of life that I actually had life-determining decisions to make, and it scared me more than I wanted to admit.

LILA

"*I*n Da Club"

"*Y*ou're really going out?" Carter pouted as he stared at me in my tight black dress. "I don't want you to go out with someone else looking so hot." His eyes traversed my body, and he gave me such a longing look that I almost canceled my plans then and there.

"What? Why not?" I gave him a look as I applied my new red lipstick. "I'm going with your sister, so it's not like it's a date or anything . . ." and then I paused to look at him and frowned. "Not that I can't go on a date, of course."

"Of course," he said, his lips thin and his face suddenly sour. "You can do what you want, but you are carrying my baby now so please remember not to drink."

"Uh-huh," I said and tried not to roll my eyes. How convenient for him to remind me just as I was headed out

140

for a night on the town. Like in the last few hours I had suddenly forgotten I was pregnant. "You know I'm not going to drink."

"I know that . . ." he said and his voice trailed off. He walked over to me then and put his arms around my waist. I felt his hands sliding up to cup my breasts. "I'd just like us to have some time for us tonight. Just the two of us." He laughed then. "I mean it's not like you can get pregnant again."

"Carter." I bit down on my lower lip and laughed as I looked up at him. "Very funny."

"We don't have to bother with a condom anymore." His eyes devoured me as I gazed at him. I could feel my resolve weakening. I wanted to stay home now. I wanted him to eat me up.

"Well, we didn't always bother with the condom, did we?" I said while giving him a slight look. Not that I was trying to blame him. I mean, I'd been just as irresponsible. I'd been taught in high school that the pull-wout method was not an effective way to prevent pregnancies, but well, I hadn't really cared that night. Apparently, neither did Carter since he made no attempt to pull out. I'd just wanted to feel him inside of me so badly. I'd been so hot for him. In fact, I was feeling even hotter for him right now as his fingers gently massaged my breasts and my nipples hardened.

"Wouldn't you rather spend the night with me?" he asked as he leaned forward to kiss me in that way he knew that I loved; gently at first, but then more insistent.

"We can still have fun when I get back," I said, feeling too prude to say fuck and too sober to say make love. I mean, the sex was hot, and I definitely had feelings for him, but I didn't want to scare him off by saying make love.

"I want to fuck you so badly, Lila," he growled as he slipped one of his hands up my dress and rested it between my legs. He obviously had no inhibitions about using the word. "Come here," he said, and before I knew what was happening he had turned me around and bent me forward so that my stomach was resting on the chair. I heard his zipper going down as he slid my panties to the side, his finger grazing my clit roughly as he rubbed me. "You're already wet," he growled excitedly, and I felt the tip of his cock rubbing against my clit, already hard. "Tell me you want me," he said as he placed himself at my opening. "Tell me you want me inside of you."

"Carter," I moaned as I closed my eyes, my body trembling in sweet anticipation. Of course, I wanted him. There hadn't been a moment since we'd met that I hadn't wanted him. And during the last week I had missed him more than I'd thought was possible and that had scared me. "We don't have time for this."

"Please," he groaned as his cock rubbed me. I closed my eyes and tried not to fall to the ground. I was so horny and ready for him. "I'll be fast."

"Is that meant to be a good thing?" I laughed slightly, and then I backed my ass up against him. "Come on then, big boy," I said, and my stomach curled as he growled behind me. I felt him sliding himself inside of me, and I cried out in ecstasy as I felt all of him deep inside of me. It was such an amazing feeling.

"Oh, how I've missed you, Lila." He held onto my hips and thrust himself back and forth inside of me, and I gripped onto the chair tightly. I could feel all of his manhood deep in me, and I screamed with pleasure as he started going even faster, and then we heard the doorbell. "Fuck," Carter groaned as he pulled out of me and zipped his pants up quickly. "My sister literally has the worst timing."

"I told you we didn't have enough time." I moaned as I straightened and looked at his annoyed petulant face. I gave him a quick kiss, and he growled.

"You could always not go."

"I'm going." I shook my head.

"Take your panties off." He lifted my dress up. "I want them."

"Carter." I blushed as his hands started to move my panties down.

"Something to keep me warm while you're gone tonight." He grinned as he pulled them all the way down, and I stepped out of them. "Coming," he shouted as the doorbell rang again. He stuffed the panties in his pocket and then hurried to the front door. "Yes?" He almost shouted as he opened the door.

"Hey, bro." Danielle sailed in, oblivious to the fact that she had just interrupted our lovemaking. "Lila, you look hot." She whistled as she walked into the room. I stared at her in her glittery silver dress, and I had to say the same. She looked like a supermodel. I'd never seen her with a full face of makeup and high heels before.

"You look beautiful," I said. "Doesn't she, Carter?" He just grunted in response as his eyes narrowed. He looked at Danielle, and then he looked at me.

"Where are you guys going tonight?" he asked, his voice suspicious. "And is it just the two of you?"

"We're going to dinner, and then we're going dancing in the East Village." Danielle rolled her eyes. "And in a nightclub, not the street."

"Aren't you two a bit old for a nightclub?" he said, and we both glared at him.

"We're in our twenties, brother dearest. Would you rather us head out to church tonight?"

"I mean if you want to go to a midnight mass or something." He grinned. "I'd have to suggest you both change though, can't be slutting it up in church."

"Carter." I walked over and hit him in the shoulder. "Are you calling us sluts?"

"Nooooo." He tried to kiss my cheek, and I ducked.

"Rude."

"I was just joking." He made a face, and Danielle laughed.

"Yeah, call him out Lila. He thinks he can be a manwhore and get away with it, but we're meant to be Virgin Mary's." And then she made a face as she realized what she'd said. "Oops, well maybe none of us are exactly virgins."

"Yeah, not quite." I laughed, not offended at all. "Shall we go?"

"Yes. I'll get the Uber." Danielle pulled out her phone and started playing some music. "You can find me in da club, bottle full of bub," she rapped along with 50 Cent as she danced around the room. Her excitement was infectious, and I started spinning my head around in time to the music.

"Go, Shorty, it's your birthday, we're going to party like it's your birthday," I sang and started dancing around as well. I looked at Carter and danced for him, swaying back and forth, my hands moving up and down his chest. He looked at me with dark eyes and a small smile on his lips. "You're a bad girl." He mouthed at me and I just winked at him.

"Uber will be here in five minutes," Danielle said in an excited voice. "I'm going to find me a man tonight."

"Yeah, girl," I said and we high-fived, and Carter's expression changed to one of annoyance again.

"Come with me a second," he said as he grabbed my hand and pulled me toward the bedroom.

"We don't have time, Carter," I said as he closed the door behind me and gave me a deep kiss.

"I know." He walked over to my drawer and started rifling through my underwear.

"What are you doing?" I frowned as he looked through my panties.

"Wear these." He pulled out a pair of plain white cotton panties and handed them to me.

"What?" I blinked at him confused.

"No way in hell am I letting you go out to a dance club with no panties on," he growled at me.

"You're the one that took my panties," I complained.

"Yeah and I'm keeping them." He smirked at me. "Put these on."

"I'm not wearing those." I shook my head. "They are so not sexy."

"You want to wear sexy panties?" He raised an eyebrow as he stared at me. "Why?"

"Carter!" I rolled my eyes at him. "Just give them to me." I sighed and pulled on the granny panties. "This so ruins the vibe of my dress and heels."

"When you get home, they'll be off anyway, so don't worry about it." He pulled me toward him, and I felt his tongue in my mouth as he ran his hands down my hair to my back. "You can still cancel."

"I'm not going to cancel." I pulled away from him.

"I know." He looked displeased. "Don't stay out all night. Don't flirt. Don't kiss anyone. Don't—" He stopped and then gave me a wry smile. "Okay, maybe I am a bit bossy."

I just smiled at him. It was funny to see him like this. Annoying as hell, but a little bit nice as well.

"I'm coming home to you, Carter."

"Good." He kissed me on the nose. "Have fun tonight."

"Are you going to stay here tonight then? Or are you going to go out?"

"I'll stay here, watch some TV if you don't mind. I want to be here when you get back home."

"I won't be out all night," I said and gave him a huge kiss. His face looked so handsome, and I was so happy that he was here. However, a part of me was really sad that he was going to be leaving me to tour Canada. I was sure that the music execs would send him a contract to sign at some point soon. And I knew that as soon as he got the contract, he'd be gone. For two whole months. To Canada and the South. Granted, it wasn't that far away, but it was still away from me. He'd be gone for two months. Two whole months. That was a really long time to be away from him. I didn't want him to go, but I didn't want to tell him that. I didn't want to stop him from pursuing his dreams. It wasn't fair.

"Uber's here." Danielle knocked on the door.

"Coming." I walked over to the vanity and grabbed my small black Chanel clutch that I'd purchased with my first big paycheck from the firm. "Bye," I said to Carter.

"Bye," he said as I walked through the bedroom door. "Have a great night, girls."

∼

"*L*ila." Dante's warm voice sounded before I saw him. "What are you doing here?"

I looked around and saw him standing with

his two cousins, Blake and Steele, both of whom were just as gorgeous as he was. It was unfair how their family genes were so perfect.

"I'm here with my friend, Danielle." I introduced Dante to my friend. She was standing next to me with her mouth slightly ajar, and a flirtatious smile on her face. However, she wasn't staring at Dante. She was staring at his cousin Steele. Interesting.

"Danielle, this is my good friend and workmate, Dante. These are his cousins, Blake and Steele Vanderbilt." I gave all three of them a quick hug. "We decided to come out dancing tonight."

"And your crazy boyfriend is okay with that?" Dante laughed, and I made a face at him.

"He's not my boyfriend, and this is his sister." I pointed at Danielle who just laughed.

"He is crazy. Trust me, I know that already." She gave the boys her hand, and I noticed that Steele held onto it for slightly longer than was necessary. Interesting.

"So what are you guys up to?" I asked, surprised to see them at a dance club. They didn't strike me as the sort of men to frequent dance clubs. I looked at them and they all grinned at me.

"We didn't come to dance, if that's what you were thinking." Dante grinned. "We're thinking about buying this club and some others owned by the same management company, so we wanted to check them out first."

"Oh, nice, cool," I said. I'd forgotten that Dante's family was super rich, even outside of his partnership at the firm. He had to be a millionaire or a billionaire or something. You'd never know it to hang out with him. He didn't act like a rich jerk, but it was in moments like this that I remembered he was dripping with gold and diamonds.

"Would you ladies like a drink?" Steele asked, but he wasn't even looking at me.

"Yes, please," Danielle said, and I just shook my head. "Not drinking."

"Oh?" Dante looked surprised. "Sober tonight."

"And the next nine months." I smiled at him.

"Nine months?" He looked confused and then it dawned on him and his eyes widened. "No way." He looked at my stomach. "You're pregnant."

"Yup." I grinned.

"Not by the jerk?" He shuddered in fake horror. At least I thought it was fake, anyways.

"Yes."

"No way." He shook his head at me and laughed. "You girls really are crazy."

"Dante." I poked him in the chest. "What does that mean?"

"Didn't you see that Carter was a big player, he didn't want a relationship, and isn't he some sort of musician?" His hazel eyes bore into mine. "And let's not forget how jealous and possessive he is, not a great combination."

"It's only because he loves her." Danielle spoke up for her brother.

"He doesn't love me." I shook my head vehemently, slightly sad at that fact. I wished he loved me, but there was no way he did. Hadn't he just told me he didn't want to marry me? My heart was still aching from hurt by that comment.

"Trust me, he does." Danielle rubbed my shoulder. "He might not know it yet, but I see the way he looks at you. He loves you." She smiled at me. "He's a big doofus that's never had to deal with emotions before. He'll get it. Eventually. I hope."

"I hope so." Dante looked doubtful. "How are you

feeling about it all?" he asked me softly, his face concerned. "You doing okay?"

"Yeah." I nodded and gave him a quick smile. "I'm good. Really good. My parents aren't super happy that I'm going to be an unwed mother, but they are still supporting me." I rubbed his shoulder. "Thanks for asking."

"Let's get lunch next week," Dante said. "We can talk more then."

"Sounds good." I smiled at him. "Are you guys still getting a drink?"

"Yeah, you guys wanna do it?" Dante asked his cousins. Blake looked slightly bored as he stood there, but Steele was grinning from ear to ear as he chatted with Danielle.

"Hello, drinks on me. Follow me, guys." Steele headed toward the side of the club, and we all followed him. I was slightly taken aback that the plan for the night had changed. I wasn't sure how much dancing we would end up doing, but I knew from our talk at dinner that Danielle was sad that she hadn't gotten to meet anyone special recently. I would let her have the evening to flirt with Steele. I didn't need to dance up a storm.

~

"You're home." Carter opened the door for me as I fiddled with my keys. He was beaming at me through sleepy eyes, and my heart expanded with love for him. I reached over and ran my hands through his hair as I walked through the door.

"What are you doing up? It's late," I said as I closed the door behind me and slipped off my heels. "Ugh, my feet are killing me."

149

"It's only three a.m." He looked at his watch. "Tsk, Tsk, Cinderella, you're back late."

"I was out dancing with my Prince Charming, ugly stepsister."

"Oh yeah?" His eyes glittered as he pulled me toward him. "So who was there tonight?"

"It was just me and Danielle," I lied, feeling guilty, but not wanting to have to get into any arguments related to Dante again. "We had a delicious sushi dinner and then went dancing."

"You guys were dancing all night long?" He looked impressed. "With each other or . . .?"

"Carter, really?" I leaned forward and kissed him. "I didn't do anything with any other guys. Even though we aren't really defined as anything, anyway," I said pointedly.

"I know." He ran his hands through my hair. "You sure look sexy," he said and then yawned widely.

"You sure look sexy too, sleepyhead." I giggled as I took a hold of his hand. "Let's go to bed and get some sleep."

"I wanted to . . ." He started, and I cut him off.

"You really have the energy for sex right now, Carter?"

"Someone's making an assumption," he said as he lightly tapped my ass. "I was going to say I wanted to talk."

"Oh, okay." I laughed and pulled my dress off as we walked into my bedroom. "Shoot," I said as I turned around to face him.

"I'm oddly turned on right now," he said. "That's a very hot see-through bra and those panties, mmm." He licked his lips. "Hello, Granny."

"Carter." I smacked him on the arm. "You're horrible."

"I know." He bit down on his lower lip and smiled. "Come to bed."

"Hold on." I removed my bra, and I heard his audible intake of breath as he stared at my naked breasts. I loved the way he reacted to my naked body. It made me feel so sexy and seductive. "Put your hands up," I said, and he did so without answering as I pulled his T-shirt off. I then put it on and clambered to the bed.

"No fair," he said as he followed me. "I thought we were both going to be topless."

"I guess you thought wrong then, sucker." I laughed.

"I still win though." He grinned at me as we climbed under the sheets. "You look sexy as hell in my T-shirt."

"Uh-huh." I blushed as he stared at me with a long intense look of desire.

"Come here." He pulled me into his arms, and I rested my head against his chest as we lay back. "I really, really missed you while you were gone. I'm so happy you're back."

"I'm happy to be back too," I said softly, my heart filling with love for him. I wanted to be able to tell him how much I adored him, but I didn't want to ruin the moment.

"So, I guess I've been thinking, and I wanted to tell you that I know I'm probably not your first choice to be a father to your child, but I will do my best to be the best dad possible. This is all really new to me, and I don't really know what I'm meant to say and do. I've never really been in a serious relationship before, and I obviously have no kids, so this is all a learning experience for me. I want to be the best man I can be for you, Lila, but I also don't know what that means in terms of what I can give. I want to be honest with you because you're really special to me. I just want us to take this day by day. Is that okay?" His voice was serious and sincere, and I knew that he must have spent the whole night thinking about what to say. His words touched me, but I was saddened but what he'd said. It wasn't good enough for me. I didn't want to take it day by day. But I knew I couldn't push him for more. This had been my own fault for getting involved with someone I knew was a playboy and not looking for a committed relationship. I'd thought I'd just wanted to have some fun as well, but I should have known better. I'd never been the sort of girl that could just hook up and not develop feelings. And now this is where I was, pregnant by a man I loved who didn't really know what he wanted from me.

"I understand where you're coming from, Carter," I said softly, and he kissed the top of my head. "I'm really tired now though, do you mind if we talk tomorrow?" I faked a long and tired yawn and closed my eyes to stop the tears that were threatening to fall.

"Okay, darling," he whispered and kissed my forehead. "Sweet dreams."

"Night, Carter," I whispered back, and my hand stroked the side of his arm as I drifted off to sleep. I breathed in his natural body odor, and I felt myself calming as I drifted off to sleep. There was nothing I could do to make him love me as I loved him, but maybe this could be enough for me.

"*P*erfect"

*L*ila's body felt warm next to mine while I held her close to me as she slept, watching her face as she dreamed dreams that I could only guess about. She moved slightly, and her leg moved over mine as she turned over, her hair now covering her face. I moved her hair back slightly so that I could see her features. She was beautiful, and my heart pounded as I lightly traced the curve of her nose and then ran my fingers across her silky eyebrows. It was 6:00 a.m. and I was wide awake, but I didn't want to move. I loved these moments when I awoke early and was able to just hold her and be with her. A part of me felt like it was creepy to just watch someone as they slept, but I dismissed it. I'd never had this feeling before. I'd never just yearned for someone with my whole being. I'd never felt so whole just being with another person.

I reached for my phone so that I could check my emails

while she slept and decided to go on Instagram. I clicked on Danielle's profile to see if she'd taken any pics from the night before, and my face froze as I saw the latest upload on the screen. It was a photo of Danielle, Lila, Dante, and two guys I didn't know. I could feel anger boiling inside of me. Had this been the plan all along? Why hadn't Lila told me Dante was going to be there? She'd told me it was just the two of them. Jealousy stirred in me as I noticed that Dante's hand was around her waist and both of them were beaming at the camera. It looked like they'd had a great night. She looked stunning in her black dress, and she looked happy.

She'd been happy to go out without me, while I'd been sitting at home waiting for her. I was about to shake her awake to confront her about the lie, but then it struck me that maybe she didn't know how to tell me. After all, we had both gone into this thinking that it was going to be a one-night stand. A fling of sorts. I'd made it very clear that I hadn't wanted anything more, so did she really owe me an explanation if she was also dating Dante? I knew that I couldn't confront her. I didn't want to upset her again, and I didn't want her to think that I was changing the tenets of our agreement. But that didn't stop me from speaking to Dante. I decided that I needed to talk to him man-to-man and figure out what was going on. He looked like the sort of guy that would be straight to the point and that was what I needed right now. I needed to know where I stood. I needed to know what the situation between them really was.

I looked for her law firm online and searched for his name in the practicing attorneys section of the site. Dante Vanderbilt popped up, and I recognized his face right away. Smug bastard. Litigation partner. Of course. I tried to suppress my anger as I copied his email address. I couldn't be rude in my email to him. I had to be polite. My grandma always used to say, "You catch more flies with honey." I sent him a quick email and asked him if he would be free to meet for a drink later that day or the next. I needed to talk to him soon, and I needed to do it before I made any decisions regarding the band touring.

I had another email from Harley and Carlos saying that I had forty-eight hours to sign the contract or the music execs were going to sign another up-and-coming band for the tour. I didn't know what to do. I had so much doubt about going. I had so much doubt about staying. I didn't know what I wanted to do. I shifted Lila in the bed and slid out of the sheets. I needed to have a shower. My heart was still racing from the photo I'd seen. I was scared to find out the truth. I was scared that she didn't want more. All this time, I'd been thinking that she had somehow trapped me. But maybe it was me that had trapped her, maybe this was something she hadn't wanted at all. Maybe I had ruined her life by impregnating her. I hadn't considered that before, but maybe instead of her having turned my life upside down, I'd turned hers on its tail.

∼

"You're up," I said as a sleepy-looking Lila walked into the living room.

"Barely." She yawned and smiled. "I'm hungry." She rubbed her stomach. "I need lots of food. I'm eating for two now."

"So then you shall have lots of food." I grinned. "Wanna go to brunch? I know this cool place called Sweet Chick. It's not far from here. I've been a couple of times with Danielle. I think you'll like it."

"Oh, I know it. It's yummy. Yes, let's go. I'll go change." She beamed and then hurried out of the room. I watched as she walked down the hallway, and I wanted to call out to her.

"Why did you lie?"

❧

"Oh, man, I want the fried chicken and waffles, and I want the breakfast burrito, and I want the ricotta pancakes." Lila licked her lips. "I'm so hungry if you couldn't tell."

"I could tell. Just a little bit." I grinned at her. "I have an idea."

"What?" She drank some of her Arnold Palmer, her eyes bright as she gazed at me.

"You get the fried chicken and waffles, I'll get the breakfast burrito and we can split them. And then we can get the pancakes on the side and share."

"Oh my God, I love you." She grinned at me excitedly. "That is the perfect plan." She reached her hand forward and squeezed mine, and my heart jumped into my throat. I wanted to tell her that I loved her as well, but I knew my declaration had nothing to do with food.

"We're going to be so full when we're done." I added some milk to my coffee. "We should do something afterward."

"I was planning on going to a bookstore to go get some baby books, if you want to come?" she said and then looked down. "I mean, you don't have to . . ."

"No, I want to come. That'll be fun." I don't know why I said it would be fun. Buying baby books didn't seem fun in and of itself, but just being with Lila was enough for me to be happy. "And then maybe we can go to Prospect Park?"

"Yeah." She nodded eagerly. "I have a frisbee. We could throw that."

"Perfect," I said. "That sounds perfect."

～

"*T*hese are the books I think we should get," Lila said as she handed me a stack of about ten books.

"Whaaaa?" I held onto the books tightly. "All of these? Really? Are you sure?"

"We want to be prepared, right? I mean, neither one of us really knows anything about babies."

"Yeah, but all these books?" I was starting to wonder when I was going to have time to practice and do my music.

"Well, my doctor said I should go to prenatal classes, and maybe you can come along to some if you want . . ." Her voice trailed off, and suddenly she looked unsure of herself. "I mean, you don't have to or anything. I was just thinking that perhaps you might want to come along, if you have time, and if you don't end up getting the contract to go to Canada."

"Yeah, that sounds cool." I rubbed her back. "Anything I can do, Lila," I said, wanting to ask her if she hated me for getting her pregnant. "I'm sorry, by the way."

"Sorry for what?" She looked at me with a confused expression. "What did you do?"

"You know."

"No, I don't?"

"You know." I looked at her belly and then she burst out laughing.

"Oh, Carter." She just shook her head. "Come on, let's go and pay."

"Okay." I followed behind her to the cash register and then felt someone tapping me on the shoulder.

"Oh my God, oh my God, are you Carter Stevens? The Carter Stevens!" A young kid about nineteen was standing behind me. "Oh shit, man, can I get a photo for my Insta?"

"Um sure."

"Damn, my friends are not going to believe it. I love The Bedroom Rockers." He grinned. "Sorry, I know I'm being so uncool right now, but you're so big in Toronto."

"Oh, you're from Canada?" I smiled back at the kid. "That's awesome."

"Yeah, my friends and I listen to underground rock bands, and we stream all your stuff on Spotify. That last album man, so cool. That's why I love indie bands. You guys can do what you want."

"Thanks, man. Yeah, we're actually thinking about signing with a label. We might even be touring in Canada soon."

"No fucking way. That would be awesome."

"Yeah, it would be. I'm just deciding whether or not to sign the contract." And as I said the words, I realized that Lila was standing right next to me and was listening to everything I was saying as was evidenced by the distraught expression on her face.

"Cool, man." The guy stood next to me and put his phone up to take a selfie of the two of us. "Wait until I tell my friends," he said and then walked away.

"Looks like you have a lot of international fans," Lila said in a stiff voice.

"Yeah, looks like it."

"So you're deciding if you want to sign the contract?

You're not waiting for them to send you the contract?" Busted!

"Well, I . . ." My voice drifted off as she gave me a stern *do not lie to me* face. Damn, I'd never seen that expression on her face before. "Yes."

"So you can go. You have the contract?"

"I don't know if this is what I should be doing right now." I nodded toward the baby books, and she sighed.

"No, Carter, you do not *not* go because of this baby. This is your dream. This has always been your dream. You have to go."

"I don't want you to feel abandoned," I said earnestly. "I don't want you to think I hit it and quit, and now you're pregnant and well, I just don't want to walk away. I like you a lot, I even lo . . . I even think that this could be something special, and I don't want to lose that by going on this tour."

"Listen to me, Carter, you're going on that tour, even if I have to forge your signature on the paperwork. And then they'll send me to jail, and our baby will be born behind bars. Do you want that? Do you want a jailbird baby?"

"Not really." I laughed ruefully. "But I still don't think that . . ."

"Sh." She put a finger on my lips. "This is an amazing opportunity. Go. If I didn't have to work, and if I wasn't a lawyer, I would jump to be in your shoes."

"You would go if you were me?"

"In a heartbeat." She leaned forward and kissed me. "You have to do this, Carter. I would never forgive myself if you didn't go. Pursue your dreams. I will still be here. I promise."

"You promise?"

"I promise. You're so talented and amazing, you have to share your music with more people." She nodded solemnly and my heart melted at the kind and loving words. She was so amazing and wonderful. I could barely believe she was real.

"Ooh, it's Ed Sheeran," Lila exclaimed gleefully as music started playing from the speakers in the store. "I love this song. I think it's called, 'Perfect'."

"Oh God, here we go," I groaned as the song started playing, but I grinned to myself; this was how I knew she was real. If she were a figment of my imagination, she wouldn't be listening to and enjoying Ed Sheeran. However, as I listened to the lyrics, I realized that this was one song that actually made sense to how I felt right now. Ed's lyrics were exactly how I felt at that moment, "I found a woman stronger than anyone I know, she shares my dreams, I hope someday that she shares my home." I knew how he felt. I loved Lila. I knew that as sure as I knew anything. I wanted to live with her. I just didn't know what was next. And I didn't know what she wanted. I was going to meet up with Dante later that evening, and once I'd spoken to him I would figure out what my next step would be.

LILA

"*S*ay You Won't Let Go"

"*H*ey you?"
"*Hey!*"
"*What you doing?*"
"*Watching TV? Are you still with Harley?*"
"*Yes, we're going to grab a drink.*"
"*Coming over after?*"
"*Don't think so tonight as I have an early morning.*"
"*Oh.*"
"*:(*"
"*:(*"
"*I'll miss you.*"
"*Then you should come over.*"
"*I would if I could, babe.*"
"*Okay.*"

. . .

*T*put the phone down and flipped the channels. Today had been an emotional one for me. The morning had started out perfectly with brunch and then going to buy the baby books. Carter had been so caring and thoughtful, but then I'd found out he actually already had the opportunity to go to Canada. I didn't care that he'd lied. In fact, it had been kinda sweet that he'd thought about staying for me and the baby, but I didn't need that sort of pressure. He would always resent me if he gave up this opportunity to expand his music career. I didn't want him to go. In fact, it made me nervous and weepy to think about him traveling across North America with a rock band and no real commitment to me. I didn't even know if he would be faithful to me. I didn't know if we were meant to be monogamous or not. We'd never really spoken about it, and I didn't want to ask him now. I must have fallen asleep because I woke up about two hours later to my phone beeping.

"Check this out." Carter had attached a photo of a cute puppy cuddling a kitten and my heart melted.

"Softy."

"That's not what you said last night."

"We didn't have sex last night."

"Oh yeah, that wasn't you. :P"

"That's not funny." I glared at the phone.

"Miss you."

"Come over."

"Early morning."

"Fine."

"Send me a selfie. I want to see your pretty face."

"You send me one."

"Fine here." He sent me a photo of himself sitting in bed

with his shirt off. He looked so hot, and I wished more than anything he was there with me.

"*Nice. :)*"

"*My turn now.*"

"*Fine.*" I took a photo of my feet and sent it to him giggling.

"Are you trying to tell me something, Lila?"

"Like what?"

"Like you want me to suck on your toes."

"Ew, no."

"*Uh-huh, freaky Lila.*"

"*Whatever, Carter.*"

"*Send me a proper pic. I want to see your face.*"

"*Magic word.*"

"*Please.*"

"*Okay, here we go. :)*" And then I snapped a quick photo and sent it to him.

"*So beautiful.*"

"*Uh-huh.*"

"*Sweet dreams, princess.*"

"*Night, Carter.*" I wanted to ask him when I would see him next, but I didn't want to be one of those pushy women. He could ask me to hang out when he wanted to see me again. He already knew I wanted to see him. I put the phone down again and then jumped up off of the couch to walk to my bedroom. I was tired and needed to go back to sleep. It had been a long weekend and I'd only just gotten back from Iowa. I had work tomorrow and needed to be up bright and early.

"*H*ey, Lila." Dante popped his head into my office. "Wanna grab lunch today?"

"I shouldn't." I looked at the stack of files on my desk. "I'm swamped today. Just going to get a sandwich. Maybe later this week?"

"Can we do today?" He gave me a warm smile. "I'll be out of the office the rest of the week."

"Really?" I frowned. "Don't you have partner meetings?"

"They got moved." He walked into the office and sat in the chair in front of my desk, leaned forward and grabbed my hands. "I want you to have lunch with me today, Lila. My treat."

"Your treat?" I raised an eyebrow. Lunches with partners were normally expensed to the firm. What was this about?

"I just think that we deserve some alone time, you know?" He stood up and walked to the door. "I won't take no for an answer. I'll meet you in the lobby at noon."

"Hmm, okay?" I watched as he walked away, a perplexed expression on my brow. What was going on with Dante? And was he flirting with me? Had Carter been right? Had Dante just been waiting for his chance with me? I groaned under my breath. I really didn't need this right now. Not at all.

~

"*W*ell, this has been absolutely yummy." I smiled at Dante weakly over the table. He'd gone all out for our lunch and we were dining at a very expensive French restaurant. I wasn't sure what was going on, but I certainly hoped he wasn't going to make an advance toward me.

"Hasn't it been great?" He reached over and grabbed my hands. "I've been meaning to tell you something, Lila."

"Yes?" Oh no, oh no, oh no.

"So, I've been thinking about you a lot and how you've been . . ." His voice trailed off as he looked to the front of the restaurant. "Oh boy," he said, and he looked at me with a worried expression.

"What?" I blinked at him and then I saw Carter had entered the restaurant and was headed toward us. Fuck! How had he known I was going to be here? Or had he conveniently chosen the same restaurant for lunch? I wanted to cry as I saw Carter approach with a furious face.

"Really, Lila?" Carter stopped in front of the table. "You're having lunch with this scumbag?"

"Carter, I . . ." I paused as I looked toward Dante's face and he was laughing. "This isn't funny," I said as I frowned. And then I noticed that Carter was laughing as well, a huge grin on his face.

"Too much?" he said as he high-fived Dante.

"Maybe." Dante grinned.

"What the hell is going on here?" I looked back and forth between the two men. Carter then dropped to his knees and my breath caught. What was going on here?"

"Lila Delilah, my darling, my one and only, I love you. I have loved you from the first moment I saw you with your sparkling brown eyes and infectious smile. You light up my life in a way I never knew was missing. I never believed in love at first sight before, but when you know, you know. I want to marry you. I want to love you forever. I want you to be the mother of my kids, and I want to adore you with every fiber of my being. I know that we don't know each other well. I know that you might not feel the same way, but I want you to give me a chance. Marry me, Lila. Let me prove to you how much I love you."

"I just don't understand." My jaw dropped as my heart raced. "What are you doing here? How did this happen?" I was rambling, but I couldn't quite believe what was happening.

"I saw Danielle's pics on Instagram from the other night. You said you'd been alone with Danielle, but then I saw good old Dante there in the photos. I knew there had to be a reason why you hadn't told me and I wanted to find out what was going on between you guys. I didn't want to get mad. I didn't want to make you have to choose between us. I didn't want you to feel like you had to be with me because you were having my baby if you were in love with him, so I met up with Dante, and I realized that you were always telling the truth, and the two of you are just friends. My jealousy got the better of me, I admit it. And I'm sorry. I understand why you lied."

"Oh Carter, I'm sorry."

"Will you marry me, Lila?" His eyes were sky blue as they gazed at me hopefully. "Do you love me?" His voice was soft and nervous.

"Oh, Carter. I love you so much." I jumped up and threw my arms around him. "Of course, I love you, you big doofus. I love you more than anything."

"Told you, dude," Dante said with a grin. "It was obvious to me from the start."

"And you'll marry me?" He held his breath as he gazed at me and I leaned forward and gave him a huge kiss.

"I love you, and I will marry you," I said, and he picked me up and twirled me around like a little kid. "I'm feeling a bit dizzy now though," I said as he finally stopped twirling and put me down.

"I have some other news." He bit down on his lower lip

and looked nervous. "I spoke to Harley and Carlos last night after I met with Dante."

"Oh, you guys met up last night?"

"Yeah." He grinned. "Anyways, Harley and Carlos spoke to the execs and they are willing to pay you to come along with us on the trip to Canada as our band attorney and Dante said he would give you three months paid vacation since you'd still be practicing law for us and the firm. That's if you decided that was something you wanted to do. I know you might not want to come and you might find it boring, but I would love to have you be a part of this experience with me."

"Are you frigging joking me?" My jaw dropped. "Is this for real?" I looked at Dante, and he just grinned at me. I threw my arms around him and hugged him. "Thank you, thank you, thank you."

"I take it that's a yes then?" Carter said with a gigantic grin.

"It's a million times yes. Yes to loving you, yes to marrying you, and yes to touring with you." I walked back over to him and took a hold of his hand. "This is going to be so amazing. I'm in shock right now. We need to celebrate."

"Yes! Want to come with us, Dante?" Carter said. "Maybe I can get Danielle to come as well. We can go to Tavern on the Green."

"I wish I could." Dante looked at his watch. "I actually have a blind date to get ready for."

"Oh? A blind date? Really?" I laughed. "No way."

"My nana set it up." He rolled his eyes. "I've never even seen her."

"Wow, so it's really, really blind."

"Yes, it is." He made a face. "Wish me luck."

"It'll be great," I said. "She'll be lucky to have met you."

"Yeah, she will be." He winked and laughed. "Okay love birds, enjoy your afternoon," he said as he made his way to the exit. "Do not come back to work this afternoon, Lila. You hear me?"

"Yes, boss." I grinned and watched as he walked away. And then I turned back to Carter and kissed him again. "I love you, Carter Stevens. You're a goof, but I love you."

"I love you too, Lila James. You're my whole world and I can't wait to make many, many babies with you."

"Of course you would say that." I wanted to roll my eyes at him, but all I felt was incredibly happy.

"I learned a new song." He looked suddenly shy. I was at the bar last night with Harley and there was a singer who started singing this song and as I listened to the words I knew that this was the song that should be our song."

"Ooh another Ed Sheeran?" I grinned at him like a dope. "You lurve Ed Sheeran now. Almost as much as you love me."

"I could never love anyone as much as I love you. And no, it's not Ed Sheeran. It's some guy called, James Arthur. Do you know him?"

"I love James Arthur." I looked into his eyes and I knew that he was talking about Say You Won't Let Go, one of my absolute favorite songs. I cradled his face and started singing. "Then you smiled over your shoulder, for a minute I was stone cold sober."

"I knew I loved you then, but you'd never know, 'Cause I played it cool when I was scared of letting go." He sang to me, his voice so raw that I couldn't stop a few tears from springing to my eyes. "I've loved you so deeply that it almost doesn't seem real." He whispered in my ear. "I never knew a feeling like this existed."

"That's not part of the song." I grinned at him.

"Sometimes you don't need a song to express whats in your heart. Sometimes the words just come naturally. Sometimes the music inside of us is even better than what we hear externally."

"Are you becoming a romantic, Carter Stevens?" I stroked the side of his face. "I have dreamed of this moment. I have waited for this moment. When I'm apart from you, I miss you so much. You're a part of me."

"In more than ways than way." He rubbed my belly and he suddenly grew very still. "We're going to have a baby, Lila. We're actually bringing another life into this world."

I just grinned at him as he leaned forward to kiss me. It seemed like everything was finally going my way. I had the man; we were getting married, and we were going to have a baby. I should have known that this was only the beginning of what was going to be a whirlwind of a ride.

The End

Thank you for reading *Along Came Baby*, there will be a sequel to this book continuing with Lila and Carter's story called, Along Came Marriage and it is available for preorder now. There will also be a book for Dante, Lila's sexy coworker called *Dante* that is also available for preorder. Turn the page to read a teaser from Dante.

DANTE TEASER

Read a from Dante on the next pages.

Preorder Dante now!

About Dante

A blind date set up by her grandmothers best friend.
A mistaken identity.
A crying baby left at her apartment

.

What could possibly go wrong for Sadie Johnson? Just about everything. She thought her week couldn't get any worse and then she went on her date and met Dante.

Dante Vanderbilt. Hot, charming, sexy, rich, and arrogant. He was the sort of man that every woman wanted to tame. Every woman except Sadie. She disliked him on sight and she let him know that right away. However that only seemed to amuse him and want her even more. Even though he assumed she was a flighty, careless single mother. Even though she let him believe that was true and that she would never want him as a stepdad to her pretend kid. He seemed to find her distaste appealing which only irritated her even more. Sadie couldn't wait to leave the date and Dante behind, only he seemed to keep popping up wherever she went.

Sadie wasn't sure what Dante wanted from her, but one thing she knew for sure was that she was in way over her head.

PROLOGUE

*T*ried to keep my cool as I stared at the man in front of me. He was perfection in every way. Tall, handsome, sexy, eyes that seemed to pierce into my soul when he gazed at me, a smile that said I want to eat you up, and his touch made promises to my body that I didn't know if he could deliver. To sum it up, when you looked at him, Dante Vanderbilt was like some sort of sex god. It almost wasn't fair. When I looked at him, I thought of rolling around in bed, sheets and legs entwined together. I imagined him gazing at me, like he was now, like I was the sexiest woman he'd ever seen in his life. But I knew for Dante, this was all a game and I knew that I had to take him down a couple of notches.

Don't get me wrong, I am just like you. I'm the girl that wants love. The girl that enjoys sex. The girl that wants hot sex with a man she loves. That loves her back. I don't like games. I don't like drama. I've never had a one-night stand. I've never done anything like this before. That might be hard to believe. I don't even really know how I got into this situation. Well, I know, but I don't know how I let it go this far. This was the roller-coaster ride that was never-ending and the ride was really only just beginning.

"Tonight is the night." Dante's voice was husky as he slowly unbuttoned his crisp white shirt. Holy damn, he was hot! "I'm going to do things to you that you've only dreamed of."

"How do you know I've dreamed of them?" I asked as I stared at his long slim tan fingers. "And how do you know I haven't done them all already?" I winked at him and smiled to myself as he paused with his buttons and gave me a sultry look. I couldn't help but stare at his tongue as he licked his lips like some hungry wolf that wanted to devour me. I swallowed hard and blushed as I thought about the things his tongue had done to me just a couple of nights before. It was if he knew just where every sensitive spot in my body was. It had been torture stopping him from actual intercourse, but I'd still orgasmed. I couldn't imagine what he could do with other parts of his body if he could take me on the roller-coaster ride of all roller-coaster rides with just his tongue.

"Well, I'll just have to make sure I find something that is new to you." He growled and I watched as he threw his shirt on the ground, like some sort of expensive hot male stripper in Vegas. Not some Channing Tatum look alike either (though I wasn't sure if he had been an expensive stripper or not in the movie; I could just remember him swinging his hips). Dante was way hotter than Channing Tatum; though I would never tell him that.

"No strings attached, right?" His voice was smooth as he stood there and I watched as he took his jeans off. I couldn't stop myself from gawking at his body. He was now naked from the waist up. He had a smattering of dark chest hair that covered his muscular pecs and ran down to his perfect abs. His skin was a golden olive tan and his hazel eyes shone like emeralds in the candlelight. I still couldn't get over how sometimes his eyes looked so green and at other times looked so brown. He was wearing a pair of white boxer briefs that left nothing to the imagination. He had a huge grin on his face and his teeth looked unnaturally white in the darkness of his room.

I stared at him wondering if I had the guts to go ahead with my plan. It was tricky because while I wanted to bring him down, I was also attracted to him. Very, very attracted to him. And I was worried that I would be the one that would pay if everything went wrong. They always say that the best-laid plans of mice and men often go awry. And I had a feeling that I could definitely be the one that would get burned in this situation. Even though I had planned everything out to go as smoothly as possible. Only I wasn't quite sure I really had the perfect plan. But right now it didn't matter. This was a risk I was willing to take.

"Right." I nodded as I licked my lips slowly, hoping desperately that I looked sexy as I did so. I walked towards him slowly, and seductively enjoying the feel of my flowy red dress brushing against my legs. "No strings attached." My voice sounded strange to my own ears. I'd never said anything like that before in my life. Had never even thought that I would ever be okay with it. However, somehow I had convinced myself that this was the way to go.

"Take your dress off," he said, his eyes looking darker now as he took a step toward me. His gaze was intense and he suddenly seemed taller, more muscular, more dangerous than he had before. A thrilling, exhilarating feeling washed over me. This was the hottest situation that I'd ever been in. "I said now, Sadie." His voice got deeper and he moved even closer. I stood there feeling like a statue as he leaned in close to me and whispered in my ear, "I said, take off your dress, sexy, or I'll do it for you." And then I felt his teeth on my earlobe nibbling and pulling it gently before his lips fell to my neck, and he kissed down my neck to my collarbone. My body was on fire and every limb was trembling in sweet anticipation. I could think of nothing but having him then. Absolutely nothing.

I stood there for a few seconds, unable to move, and then his hand reached and cradled my breast and I felt like I was about to explode.

"I know your secret," he whispered.

"What?" I blinked at him, my heart freezing. He couldn't possibly know, could he?

"I know your secret," he said again with a smirk. "But what you don't know is that I have one as well."

DANTE CHAPTER 1

*O*ne Month Ago

"*S*adie, I've got you a date for Saturday," my grandma exclaimed dramatically as soon as I answered the phone.

"Hello, Grandma Louise, and no thank you." I sighed into the phone in exasperation. "I have no time for a date on Saturday."

"Sadie Johnson, I've gone out of my way to get you this date, so you don't wind up . . ."

"Alone and childless, I know, I know." I groaned into the phone. "Grandma, I'm twenty-eight, I've got plenty of time."

"That's what you young ladies think nowadays. In my day, if you weren't betrothed by seventeen, there was a problem."

"Grandma, I thought you and Grandpops met when you were twenty-two?"

"Well, you know . . ." her voice trailed off. "Anyways, my best friend Addie set it up. You'll be going on a date with one of her grandsons."

"Addie?" I said in a confused voice. "Who's Addie? I've never even heard of her before."

"Don't tell me you've forgotten my best friend Addie?" Grandma sounded appalled and mumbled on about something else, but I was no longer paying attention because the kids from downstairs were throwing water balloons through my open kitchen window.

"I've never heard of her before, Grandma."

"Well you must have forgotten. Anyway, her grandson Dante Vanderbilt is a very eligible bachelor. And quite the looker as well."

"Grandma Louise, I'm not interested." I sighed. "If he's so great, why is he single?"

"You know someone could say that about you as well, Sadie." Her voice was stern. "Now, one little date is not going to hurt you, is it?"

"Grandma, we'll talk later. I have to go." I hung up the phone quickly before she could protest and spend the next thirty minutes trying to guilt me into going on the date with this random guy like some loser. "Brandon, Dylan, and Brody," I screamed as I ran to the window and looked down to the garden. "Stop it."

"Stop what?" Brody's muddy face gazed up at me innocently, his bright blue eyes gleaming, as he held a red balloon in his wet hand. His little five-year-old face was adorable, but I was no longer deceived by his childish wiles. He was a terror through and through, along with his brothers.

"You know what," I growled and shook my head at him. "I'm coming down to talk to your mom."

"No, we'll stop," Dylan exclaimed panicked. He was

smart enough to know that getting his mom involved wouldn't be a good thing. At six years old, he was the oldest of the brothers, but he was definitely not the boss.

"Too late," I exclaimed as I backed away from the window with a hidden grin. I grabbed my keys and headed out the door to the downstairs apartment so I could speak to the boy's mom, Cara, who happened to be my best friend. I had no intention of complaining about the boys though; I wanted to bitch about Grandma Louise and my new job instead. I didn't bother locking the door because we lived in the same house and everyone in the house was welcome in my upstairs apartment. It was a unique housing situation, but one that worked well for us. Cara's dad had bought the house for her when her childhood boyfriend had left her and their three kids. She rented out the top floor to me and I got a bit of a discount in the rent for babysitting the kids every now and again.

"Cara, where are you?" I said as I walked down the stairs and into her living room. It was full of toys and I trod carefully across the floor, making sure to pay attention to the junk in front of me because I didn't want to trip up and twist my ankle like I'd done the last time I'd been down there.

"In the kitchen," she called out and I hurried to the kitchen hoping that she was baking cookies. I was in the mood for chocolate chip cookies and milk or a shot of whiskey. Either one would do. "How's it going, doll?" She grinned at me as I walked into the room. Her long frizzy red hair was a mess and she had a streak of something on her face, but she looked as happy as ever.

"I'm good," I said and looked around to see what I could grab to snack on. "But do you know what your brats are up to?" I mumbled before I remembered that I wasn't going to tell on them. I really was the worst *aunt*.

"Water balloons?" I nodded, and she groaned as she looked at me. "Oh shit, did they get you with them?"

"Well, they tried," I said with a small smile. "They threw them through the window and missed me, so I guess I'm the winner."

"Want a glass of wine?"

"Do you have red?"

"What sort of question is that?" She walked over to the corner of the kitchen and opened a cupboard and before I could blink she was pulling out a bottle of wine. "Merlot good?"

"Beggars can't be choosers," I said and I walked over to grab two wine glasses while she opened the bottle. Merlot wasn't my favorite, but at the end of the day, wine was wine. "So guess what?" I said dramatically as I turned to her.

"Uhm," she groaned as she shook her head, ever the exasperated mom. "If it has anything to do with Brandon, Dylan, or Brody, I don't want to know right now."

"It has nothing to do with them," I said, already having conveniently forgotten the water balloon incident. "Grandma Louise called me."

"Oh Lord, what has she done now?" She handed me a glass and grinned widely. She knew Grandma Louise well. "Has she started another sex line or is she selling bingo tickets to her local ladies club?"

"Don't." I shook my head as I gulped down a huge sip of wine. Grandma Louise always had some scheme going on and I wasn't sure if she actually knew what she was doing or not. Last year, she'd gotten the idea to start a party-line with her friends. She claimed she didn't understand what it meant and thought she was just offering phone calls to military men who were lonely and stationed overseas and just wanted someone to talk to. I asked her why she had a late-night ad on the local TV station if she thought the guys were overseas and then she started talking about how dementia ran in the family. "I still can't believe she was rigging the weekly bingo sessions by creating winning cards and selling them at a discount to members of the club."

"I can't believe people were paying twenty dollars to win a bingo pot of ten dollars." Cara and I made eye contact and started giggling. "Who knew people wanted to be winners that badly?"

"Apparently Grandma Louise knew." I shook my head and my voice softened. "Ever since Grandad Fred died five years ago, she's been doing all sorts of craziness, but I can't help but love her."

"So what's her newest idea?" Cara leaned forward on her white marble island excitedly.

"She's set me up on a date." I took another huge gulp of wine and groaned. "Kill me now."

"Wow, a date?" Cara looked intrigued. "With who."

"With her new best friend, Addie's, grandson."

"At least it's not her new best friends grandfather. Though maybe you'd have a connection with someone a bit older."

"Cara." I glared at her but couldn't stop myself from agreeing with her. Grandma Louise was a loose cannon. You never knew what craziness she would think up. And men could have kids until they died, so age wouldn't be a factor if she just wanted me to give her great grandkids. "I'm not dating a grandfather, and I sure as hell don't want to go on a date with some rando's grandson. God, I bet he's a huge loser. Who goes on a date their grandma set up?"

"Uhm . . ." Cara pointed at me and I just made a face at her. "At least you're getting to go out on dates." She sighed. "Between the boys, my job, and my dad, I don't even have time to think."

"I'm sorry, Cara." I leaned forward and grabbed her fingers. "You know I'm here to help whenever I can."

"I know, you're the best." Cara nodded. "So do you know what this guy looks like?"

"Nope, but what do most guys that live in their grandma's basement look like?"

"Does he really live in his grandma's basement?" Cara's jaw dropped. "Like some sort of *Criminal Minds* psycho?"

"Exactly like a *Criminal Minds* psycho." I nodded and then laughed slightly. "Well, I don't know that officially, but you know what I mean."

"Oh, Sadie." Cara put her glass down and got back to seasoning her chicken drumsticks. "Do you want to stay for dinner?"

"Yeah, that would be nice." I smiled at her. "Want me to make a salad?"

"Please." She nodded. "Not that those terrors will eat any of it though." She poured half a bottle of ketchup on the drumsticks. "I'll be lucky if they eat these. All they ever want is chicken nuggets."

"Boys!" I exclaimed as I went to the fridge and took out a head of lettuce, some tomatoes, a cucumber, and some carrots.

"So tell me about the new job. How's it going?"

"Ugh." I groaned as I placed the produce on the countertop and grabbed a bowl, a cutting board, and a sharp knife. "I swear my boss is Cruella de Vil?"

"Oh?" Cara gave me a curious look. "Do explain."

"This lady is the most over-the-top, meanest person I've ever met." I pouted. "She also hates all dogs. Like, tell me how you can hate dogs?"

"How do you know she hates dogs?"

"She told me she hates dogs when we saw one walking past the coffee shop the other day." I rolled my eyes. "She literally pointed out the window, screwed up her nose and said I can't stand those stinky creatures, can you?"

"What did you say?"

"I just sipped my latte," I said as I took another gulp of wine. "I can't afford to tell her the truth. I need this job."

"So what exactly are you doing for her?" Cara covered the chicken with aluminum foil and started peeling potatoes. "She's like a millionaire, right?"

"Billionaire." I sighed. "Well her late husband was a billionaire and now she has all his money. And she wants to invest in art. So she's hired me to go around to all the museums in New York City and pick out my favorite pieces so that she can bid on them and buy them."

"What? Are they for sale?"

"Girl, who knows?" I rolled my eyes. "She's totally oblivious. I mean really?"

"Well, that doesn't sound like such a hard job." Cara looked at me hopefully.

"I have to report back to her every other day on pieces I recommend. And list all the reasons why I think they will be a good investment. Like how the hell am I supposed to know?"

"How did you get this job again?"

"I told her I studied Art History." I made a guilty face and I could feel my face growing red. "And I mean I did take some history classes and I took that one painting class."

"Oh my God, Sadie." Cara burst out laughing and she just shook her head. "You don't know the first thing about art."

"That's not true. I know a little bit." I wrinkled my

nose. "And by a little bit, I mean I can identify the Mona Lisa, like ninety-nine percent of the planet."

"Oh, Sadie," Cara spoke to me as if I were one of her sons. Completely exasperated, but with love. "You know lying never gets you anywhere."

"Well, I didn't really lie and it did get me somewhere. It got me this job." I grabbed the glass and gulped down what seemed like half of the glass of wine. "And that allows me to pay you rent."

"Girl, I don't want you to work a job that you hate just to give me money." Cara's face was serious. "Quit and look for something you really want with a nice boss."

"Girl, I love you, but you have three sons and Christmas is coming up." I shook my head. "There's no way, I'm going to be a deadbeat on you right now."

"You're not a deadbeat."

"Shh." I put my hand up. "We're not going to have this conversation. I'm still looking for new jobs, but for now, I'll play the art aficionado."

"Oh, Sadie." Cara put her glass down. "I'm so irresponsible. I should not be drinking right now."

"Sweetie, you need the wine to deal with those brats." I laughed as I looked around the kitchen. It looked a lot messier than normal and as I paid closer attention to Cara, her appearance seemed to be more frazzled. "Hey, is everything okay?"

"It's fine." She nodded and then sighed. "Well kinda. You know I love my job."

"I know and heaven knows why." I made a face. "Accounting was never my thing."

"Well, they have me working nights." She sighed. "We're auditing a couple of hotels in this chain that is being considered for purchase by some billionaire hotshot and well nights are the only time we can get access to all the files and not be in the way."

"That sucks."

"Yes, it does." She rubbed her eyes. "I'm barely keeping up and I just don't know what to do with the boys."

"I'll babysit anytime, you know that, right?"

"I know, between you and Dad, I'm so blessed. I just feel bad." She looked away from me and it looked to me like she was blinking furiously; as if she was about to cry.

"Something else is going on. Do you want to talk about it?" I asked her as I walked closer to her. "Cara?"

"I just didn't think this would be my life." She gave me a small smile. "Don't get me wrong, I love my life, but I just didn't think this was where I would be."

"I know, girl." I nodded my understanding. "I didn't think this was where I'd be either."

"Go on that date with that guy," she urged me suddenly. "Maybe it will be fun."

"Really?" I shook my head. "What is going to be fun about a date with some crusty guy my grandma set me up with?"

"Maybe you'll at least end up with an orgasm for your troubles." Cara winked at me and I groaned.

"You're joking, right?" I laughed incredulously. "You think I should have a one-night stand? With a guy I've never even seen or met before."

"What can it hurt?" She grinned widely. "I mean if he has no teeth or is butt-fuck ugly, then no. However, if you think he's hot, just go for it."

"Won't that ruin my chances at having a relationship with him?"

"Do you want a relationship with him?"

"No," I said adamantly. "I'm in no place to have any sort of relationship right now. Well, if Mr. Right came along, maybe, but I'm almost sure this guy is not Mr. Right."

"What's his name?"

"I think Grandma Louise said his name is Dante."

"Dante." Sadie nodded excitedly. "Yes, that's the perfect name for a hot stallion."

"Hot stallion?"

"Yeah, someone to go wild and crazy with."

"What's wild and crazy, Mom?" Dylan's voice interrupted our conversation and I could feel my face growing red.

"Something you should never be," Cara said smoothly without skipping a beat as she winked at me. "Now go and get your brothers and clean up. Dinner is nearly ready."

"Yes, Mom," Dylan said and went running. "Brandon, Brody, dinner is ready. Mom said to get washed up and come now or no brownies."

"Brownies?" I asked Cara with a tilt of my head as she just shook hers.

"That's his way of trying to guilt me into making them brownies." She rolled her eyes. "Not about to happen, buddy."

"Oh, ha-ha. Kids." I giggled.

"Just wait until you have them." Cara took a deep breath. "You'll see, they are a handful."

"Trust me, I already know." I laughed as I grabbed the wine bottle and poured myself another glass. Dylan, Brandon, and Brody may not have been my biological kids, but sometimes they really seemed like they were.

"Sadie, Sadie is that you?" Grandma Louise's voice was almost shouting into the phone and I frowned as I listened to the loud sounds of pumping music blaring in the background.

"Yes, Grandma," I said patiently, knowing she knew exactly who it was. "Where are you?"

"Is that why you called me, Sadie Johnson? To ask where I am?"

"No, Grandma." I rolled my eyes, knowing she was most probably at a casino with some of her friends. "I'm just jealous that you seem to have more of a life than me." Which was one hundred percent the truth.

"Well, I am trying to help you get a life," Grandma Louise said and then she gasped. "Darn it, I needed one more cherry." Yup, Grandma Louise was playing the slots. Penny slots if I wasn't mistaken.

"Well, I'm calling to say that I'll accept that date with Dante on Saturday night."

"I thought you would. He's a very good-looking young man," she said approvingly.

"Well, I've never seen him, so hopefully he really is good-looking."

"Trust me, Sadie, and if Addie is being honest, then he's quite well-off as well."

"What do you mean if she's being honest? I thought she was your best friend?"

"Now, now, Sadie. Don't start going all *Columbo* on me." She paused. "Though that Peter Falk was quite a looker. You'd be so lucky to get a man like him with your attitude. You girls these days . . ."

"I'm going to go now, Grandma Louise," I said trying to keep my patience. "Just let me know the plan for Saturday and I'll be there." Normally I would have just told her to give him my number so that he and I could set it up, but with all the stress I was feeling related to my lack of funds, sucky new job, and love life, I just didn't want to deal with it. Let them sort it out and I would show up. Maybe it wouldn't be absolutely horrible. Just maybe.

DANTE CHAPTER 2

"Five pounds, really?" I exclaimed to myself as I got off the scale and tried to erase the flashing numbers from my mind. "How the heck did I gain five pounds in one week?" I looked at my reflection in the mirror to see how evident it was that I was now gaining weight instead of losing it. My 5"8 height made it so that I could carry a few extra pounds without looking like I'd swallowed an elephant, but I could still tell that my stomach and thighs looked a little too juicy for my liking. I stared at my face and ran my hands down my long brown hair and wondered if I should cut it to a short bob. No, I thought to myself, not with my chubby cheeks. My brown eyes stared back at me, looking slightly tired and I remembered that I had a new cucumber facemark that I was going to try to see if they removed the dark circles. All in all, I didn't look horrible; in fact, I was quite pretty. I just wasn't as skinny as I wanted to be. "Ugh, I just can't believe it." I said as I got on the scale again to double check the scale had given me the correct weight. "Five more pounds. How? How?" I cried out dramatically, feeling sorry for myself.

"Cupcakes." I heard a giggle from outside the bathroom door and I frowned. I quickly walked to the door and flung it open. There sitting outside my bathroom door, playing with a toy truck was Dylan.

"What are you doing, Dylan?" I frowned as I stared at his chocolate stained face. Though I knew he had a point. I had been eating far too many delicious cupcakes as of late. I put it down to stress; even though I knew stress eating was the worst for my body.

"Playing." He held up his small red truck as if to say *duh*.

"Why are you playing up here?" I questioned him, not that I really minded. Dylan was like family to me. It was just sometimes I liked my privacy. Especially at times when I was in the bathroom weighing myself.

"'Cause." He shrugged his little shoulders and jumped up. "So you got any more cupcakes?"

"No, I don't." I shook my head at him and tried to give him my sternest face. He really was the most incorrigible little boy.

"'Cause if you give them to me that will help you with the extra pounds." He grinned at me and I glared at him; even though I knew it was not really the right thing to glare at little boys, but I knew that Cara wouldn't judge me for it. She glared at him like no one's business.

"Dylan, it is very rude to go around talking about a woman's weight," I chided him. "This is a lesson you should learn from a young age." I felt proud of myself for introducing him to a life lesson instead of getting mad at him like I wanted to. "You don't talk to women about their weight. You don't ask them how much they weigh or try and guess how much they weigh and you sure don't tell them why you think they gained weight." I paused then and considered something. "Unless, of course, you are a personal trainer or a doctor. Then you can because it will be a part of your job," I concluded, feeling even more proud of myself. Perhaps, I should become a teacher. I seemed to have a knack for talking to kids. Maybe I was the kid whisperer or something?

"But you asked how you gained five pounds," he protested and he just looked at me like I was an idiot. Maybe I wasn't the kid whisperer after all. I stared back and him and he started giggling and I could have sworn that he was staring directly at my stomach. Little bugger.

"I didn't ask you." I made a face. "I was in the bathroom and . . ."

"I'm thirsty." He interrupted me. "I want milk."

"That's not how you politely ask for milk." I shook my head at him. I was going to have to talk to Cara about making sure her kids had manners and respected my privacy. This was getting ridiculous. "Maybe go back downstairs and ask your mom?"

"Mom sent me up. She asked if you could babysit us tonight because she has to go into work." He ran his truck across the floor. "Vrooom . . . vroooom."

"Tonight?" I groaned. "I can't tonight. I have a date. She knows that." I had finally told Grandma Louise that I would meet her *best friend's* grandson and now I needed to look after the brats? What was Cara thinking? Had she forgotten?

"That's okay," Dylan said as he held up his truck. "I'll tell Mom that her boss will have to fire her after all because you can't take care of us 'cause of your date."

"Dylan . . ." I stared at the little boy shrewdly. Was he really trying to pull a guilt trip on me? Was it even possible for someone that young to be so manipulative? He was only six after all. I thought back to an old movie I'd watched on TV called *The Good Son* and wondered if perhaps, Dylan could be a little psychopath, but then I just shook my head and rolled my eyes. Even I knew I was being overly dramatic at that thought.

"Yes, Auntie Sadie?" he said in his most innocent voice, his big blue eyes shining at me as if he were a precious angel. I wasn't deceived though. I'd known Dylan since before he was born and he was no angel. He was no psychopath, but he was no angel either.

"Nothing." I shook my head and sighed. "Let's go downstairs and let me speak to your mom and see what I can do about tonight."

"Okay." He jumped up and grinned. "Can we get pizza, please? Ham, pineapple, mushrooms, pepperoni, and extra cheese."

"Pizza?" I looked at his little face and shook my head at him. "There are no words, Dylan, absolutely no words."

"No words for what?" he asked innocently and then put his small hand in mine. "Do you know what I love most about you, Auntie . . ."

"Nope." I put my hand up. "You're not going to guilt trip me into getting you pizza." And then, because I couldn't help myself, I gave him a quick hug. "You're going to break a lot of hearts when you're older, Dylan," I said with a quick laugh as he grinned at me and then he pulled away from me and went running down the stairs.

"Mom, Mom, Auntie Sadie said she can look after us and we can get pizza tonight." He went screaming in excitement and all I could do was roll my eyes as I followed him down to the lower level of the house trying to figure out exactly what was going on.

~

"Sadie, I know you have your date tonight." Cara's face looked despondent as we sat in her living room and chatted. The boys were playing in their bedrooms for once and I watched as she played with her fingers nervously. "And I wouldn't ask, but Dad is out of town and I can't find a babysitter that's available."

"I know you didn't plan this." I sighed. "I'm just supposed to meet Dante in a couple of hours." I ran my hands through my long, dark brown hair. "I don't even have his number to call and cancel on him." I bit down on my lower lip. "And Grandma Louise would kill me if I stood him up."

"You're meeting him at the coffee shop, right?" Cara asked me thoughtfully.

"Uh huh." I nodded. "Grandma Louise wanted us to meet at some steak house, but I told her no way. I'll meet him for a coffee and if I like him, I'll casually suggest we can continue on for dinner." I made a face. "No way, I'm getting stuck on a three-hour dud date with some loser just for a free steak."

"You're going to the Peets? Next to Ice Cone King?" she asked me and I could see something was ticking in her brain.

"Yeah?" I nodded.

"So what if . . ." She made a face. "And I know this is not the ideal situation. But what if you took the boys. They could sit in Ice Cone King, they have seats at the front and you could sit outside the Peets. They have those nice Adirondack chairs now."

"Oh, they do?" I asked slowly, processing what she had just said. Could I really go on a date with three kids? Granted the kids wouldn't be on the date with me, but they would be right there watching.

"I know it wouldn't be ideal." Cara bit down on her lower lip and I could tell she looked stressed. "I hate to ask this of you, Sadie, and I wouldn't go in if I thought I could get away with it." Her voice sounded upset and I reached out to squeeze her hands.

"Hey, it's not a problem." I gave her a wide smile and pretended that it sounded like a great idea. "It's only a first date as well, so we won't even be out long. I'll be able to keep an eye on them. Don't worry about it." I didn't want her to feel stressed. Cara was an amazingly positive and upbeat person, but I knew that it wasn't easy being a single mother of three at twenty-eight. And her kid's dad wasn't in the picture at all. He was such a deadbeat. It made me mad just to think about how he'd just left and didn't even see his kids. "It'll be fine."

"Are you sure?" Cara's face still looked concerned. "I really don't want to ruin your first date in ages."

"It'll be fine," I said to her. "Trust me. I'm sure it will be fine."

~

"What are you going to do with the drunken sailor? What are you going to do with the drunken sailor? What are you going to do with the drunken sailor? Early in the morning." Dylan was singing loudly in the backseat, accompanied by Brody and Brandon.

"Pull down his pants and suffocate the ants now. Pull down his pants and suffocate the ants now. Pull down his pants and suffocate the ants now. Early in the morning." Brody was really getting into it as he wiggled around in the back seat. I peered in the rearview mirror of the car and sighed to myself. The kids were already super hyped-up and I didn't think that they needed a sugar rush from the ice cream to come. It was going to be a long night.

"Come on, Auntie Sadie." Dylan tapped on my shoulder as he began another round of singing and I couldn't stop myself from joining them.

"Pull down his pants and suffocate the ants now, pull down his pants and suffocate the ants now. Pull down his pants and suffocate the ants now early in the morning," I sang and then stopped as I noticed Dylan pretending to be drinking from a beer bottle and I started to feel guilty. "Hey kids, let's sing something else. I don't know if this is an appropriate song for you guys to be singing."

"Why not, Auntie Sadie? You're the one that taught us the song," Dylan said, ever the voice of reason. I swear he should join the FBI when he's older with all his questions.

"Well, I know I taught you the song." I paused for a few seconds, but I don't know that it's appropriate for you guys to be singing it. And pretending to be drinking beer." I looked at them and then just shook my head. "But I guess your mom already knows that I've taught it to you. So it's fine." They just grinned at me and I sighed wondering what sort of example I was to them. "Oh, shit," I said, as I realized that I'd passed my stop on the highway. "Hold on, guys," I said as I sped up to take the next exit and turn around. "Man. I'm going to be late," I muttered as I looked at the time on my dashboard. I pulled up to the next exit. And then turned around so that I could pull off at the right exit. I made it to the parking lot within five minutes and breathed a sigh of release as I realized we were still early. I parked and jumped out of the car and then opened the backdoors to let the boys out. As we walked to the ice cream shop, I was happy to see that it was a nice day outside, and even though it was a Saturday evening it wasn't that busy. If it had been raining or too crowded, it would have been a hot mess.

"Okay, guys, so we've discussed the plan, right?" I stopped outside of the ice cream shop and looked at the three boys sternly. They all had looks of extreme excitement on their face. It wasn't too often that they gotten taken out for ice cream treats where they got to pick whatever they wanted.

"Yes, Auntie Sadie," they chorused, looking cherubic, their chubby little faces beaming up at me. The three of them almost looking like triplets as they were so close in age.

"So remember we're going to go into the ice cream shop now. I'm going to be in the coffee shop right next door meeting a friend. I will also be sitting outside, watching you."

"You mean a date." Dylan grinned.

"Yes, Dylan."

"I want a chocolate fudge brownie," Brody said, not caring to listen to me talk anymore. He just wanted to eat.

"I want pizza," Brandon said.

"We're going to get pizza when we get home, Brandon. First ice cream and then pizza. And you guys have to be good. Remember you told your mom, you would be good."

"We're always good, Auntie Sadie," Dylan said with a sweet smile and I just nodded at him, knowing that now was not the time to remind him of all the times that they hadn't been good.

"Yes, yes." I nodded and my heart started racing as I looked at the time on my watch. I had fifteen minutes before Dante was meant to show up. "Let's go in and get your ice cream guys and then we can get you seated," I said as I opened the door to the store, wondering if this was a really bad idea. "Also guys, just remember that my friend." I paused and looked at Dylan. "Well, my date . . . well, this is the first time I'm meeting him and he doesn't know that you guys are going to be there."

"Why not?" Brandon asked with a frown.

"Doesn't he like us?" Dylan asked and I shook my head quickly.

"He doesn't know you guys and I don't want you all to meet him until I know if he's a nice guy. Now, come on, choose what you want quickly. It's the first date and I do not want to scare this guy off by introducing him to three kids."

"Why would you be scaring him off, Auntie Sadie?"

"No reason," I said and gave Dylan a smile and hug. I didn't want them to feel like they were unlovable. I was already worried that they were getting to the age where they were starting to ask more and more questions about their dad. Sometimes I spoke to them, well especially, Dylan, as if they were adults, but I knew that they weren't and I wanted to be careful of their feelings.

"Hey guys, you're going to have your ice cream and I'm going to grab a coffee and meet with him. I'm going to be really quick and then we're going to go."

"I thought you said that you wanted to get a free steak out of it," Dylan said innocently, and I frowned. Had he been eavesdropping when I'd been talking to his mom?

"No Dylan." I shook my head. "I'm just getting a quick coffee."

"Okay," they all chorused politely. That really should have been my first sign that the night was not going to go as planned. I could even tell from the look on Dylan's face that he wasn't just going to sit patiently outside, but I was too preoccupied with other things to allow my instincts to set in and warn me of the impending drama.

"Oh, my word," I mumbled to myself as I watched the most gorgeous man I'd ever seen in my life walk toward me with a sexy saunter. He was six foot four and extremely muscular. He had dark brown silky hair that had that sexy tousled look that said he'd just stumbled out of bed. His hazel-green eyes were stunning and I as I stared at him, I watched as they turned from looking green to brown and back to green again. A light sexy stubble adorned his chiseled face and he wore a smile that was made to bedazzle as he stared at me. His stride was confident and I watched as his arms swung back and forth; strong arms and hands that looked like they knew exactly what they were doing at all moments. I could feel my body growing hot and nervous as he approached. Shit, this man was gorgeous and I already hated him. Anyone that good-looking and confident had to be an asshole. Or a psychopath. I mean, why was he going on a blind date with me if he was so well put together? I knew I was being unfair to him, but there was something about the cocky smile on his face that both turned me on and infuriated me.

"Sadie?" he asked with a smirk as he finally reached up to me outside of the coffee shop, his lips turning up slightly as he studied my frazzled appearance.

"Yes, David?" I lied. I knew his name was Dante. Obviously, I knew his name was Dante, but David slipped out so easily. I just wanted to put him in his place. It wouldn't hurt him to be brought down a peg or two. But damn, his lips were so pink and luscious as they curled up in an amused fashion. Why did he have to be so sexy? He was pretty much sex on legs. I could feel my stomach fluttering just thinking about how hot he was. "It is David, right?" I said again, pretending to look unsure and slightly confused. It didn't work though; I'm no actress. If anything his smile grew wider and his gaze more intense.

"Dante actually, but you can call me David if you prefer." He tilted his head down briefly as if to say I could do whatever I wanted.

"Why would I prefer that?" I asked in my most saccharine voice as I studied his attire. He was wearing a dark navy blue suit and a forest green tie that brought out the green in his irises. The color combination shouldn't have worked, but it did and he looked suave and handsome and completely out of my league. I brushed back my messy dark locks from instinct, not because I cared and tried not to look down at my faded blue jeans and white T-shirt that had a chocolate syrup stain on it from the ice cream shop. Obviously, I had not gotten the memo that we needed to dress up. But who dressed up for a coffee date? I mean, a suit? A sudden loud giggling caught my attention and I quickly looked to the right toward the ice cream shop and gazed over at the table where the boys sat. My eyes narrowed as I saw them sitting there eating their ice cream greedily and staring at me with delight in their beady little eyes. I couldn't believe what a hot mess of a day this was already turning out to be and I certainly didn't need them giggling and watching me make a fool of myself.

"I just thought that perhaps you would prefer to call your date by the right name?" Dante said gaining my attention again. He shrugged and as I turned back to look at him he looked down into my eyes with another curl of his lip. "Or perhaps the name doesn't matter to you?" He could tell I'd been distracted, but I knew he thought it was from disinterest.

I just stared at him for a few seconds, not knowing how to respond. We'd already gotten off to a very bad start. Just great. "Nice to meet you and make your acquaintance, Dante," I said finally, and I watched as he opened his arms to give me a hug. I was surprised at the gesture. He didn't seem to be the sort to go for hugs, but I was determined to put my best foot forward and hopefully turn the date around. I mean he was a hottie, after all, and my early judgments of him were unfair. I mean I didn't even know him yet. I stepped forward and put my arms around him and he squeezed me tightly for a few seconds before letting go. His body was hard and warm next to me and I felt a light tingle as my body pressed into his. I looked up into his eyes as I pulled away and the twinkle I saw made me blush.

"You too, Sadie. I've heard all about you from my Nana Addie."

"Really?" I gave him a doubtful look. "I haven't heard much about you from my Grandma Louise. Even though she claims to be best friends with your nana," I continued, rambling on as I was starting to feel nervous.

"Okay, phew." He started laughing then and winked at me. "I was lying. I don't really know anything about you, Sadie Johnson. Nana said she wanted it to be a surprise."

He paused as he shook his head. "And to be honest, I was also taken aback by this friendship with your grandma. I'd never heard of her before and I've met almost all of Nana's friends by now." He grinned. "She parades her grandsons around like trophies to all her friends." He laughed then. "But I digress."

"It is all very strange," I agreed and wondered if perhaps I'd judged him too quickly. Maybe he was a nice guy with a great sense of humor after all. And if he was close to his nana, that was a great sign. "I'd never heard of your nana or you before last week, but I figured I'd accept the date to make my grandma happy."

"So what makes a good-looking girl like you accept a blind date?" He cocked his head to the side and looked me up and down slowly, his eyes taking in every inch of my body in a very obvious way. I was taken aback by his boldness. Who the hell did he think he was?

"Sorry, what?" I asked him, blinking rapidly as I tried to keep my tone even. I was not in the mood to deal with any chauvinistic pigs right now. And while I'd appreciated his build in his suit, I hadn't fucked him with my eyes, had I?

"What makes a good-looking girl like you accept a blind date?" he repeated as if he didn't realize how offensive he was being. "Like what are your faults?" He grinned at me. "What should I be wary of?"

"I could ask you the same thing," I said as I tried not to roll my eyes at him. It hadn't even been five minutes and I was already back to my initial impression of him. He was a jerk.

"I'll be honest," he said as he stood there. "I don't ever want to get married," he said watching my face carefully. "That seems to turn a lot of women off."

"Okay," I said, wondering if Grandma Louise knew

that. There was no way she knew that she'd set me up with a guy that never wanted to get married. "I'm sure that doesn't rule out any sort of dating though." And I knew that for a fact. He was, unbiasedly, gorgeous. One of the best looking men I'd ever seen in my life and based on his expensive-looking leather shoes and Rolex watch, he obviously wasn't hurting for any money. Not that I cared.

"It doesn't," he agreed. "It just means that girls go a little crazy when they realize I'm not looking for a relationship."

"You're not looking for a relationship or just marriage?" I asked as I stared into his hazel eyes, that now looked more green. They were mesmerizing and I could feel myself falling into some sort of handsome man spell. Why was he telling me all of this so early on?

"Well, neither really. I don't have time for a relationship and I don't want marriage," he said and I watched as he ran his hands through his short black hair casually as if that were the most normal thing he could tell his date during the first five minutes of their meeting. "Is that a problem?"

"Why would that be a problem?" I said and shook my head. I could feel my hair moving back and forth as I tilted my head up at him. "I couldn't care less if you want a relationship or not."

"Oh . . . you're okay with just having casual fun?" His lips twitched slightly and I wanted to ask him what was so funny. I also wanted to call Grandma Louise and ask her if she knew she'd set me up with a playboy. What was she thinking?

Cara's words also crossed my mind. Maybe he was the perfect guy to have a one-night stand with. He was, most certainly, the best looking man I'd ever gone on a date with. The absolute best looking. I could only imagine he'd be dynamite in bed if the way his hands had rubbed my back during our first hug was anything to go by.

"What are you thinking about, Sadie?" Dante's voice interrupted my thoughts and I blushed as I looked up at him. His eyes were twinkling and gazing into mine as if he knew exactly what I'd just been thinking. "Have I said too much too soon? I hope I haven't put you off. I am happy to meet with you, but I thought I should be honest right off the bat," he said seriously.

"I, uh, I . . ." My voice trailed off as I suddenly noticed Dylan getting up from his seat and coming toward us. I watched as he ran up to us from the ice cream shop next door, his face a mess of chocolate syrup and whipped cream.

"Dylan, is everything okay?" I exclaimed and grabbed the little boy to pull him closer to me, aware that Dante's eyes were on me like a hawk now, wondering what was going on.

"Who's this?" Dante asked me, his eyes darting back and forth from me to Dylan, trying to figure out our connection. The smirk and sexy look were gone from his face and he suddenly looked at me with a very confused expression. I could feel my stomach dropping as his eyes narrowed and he stared at my face.

"Who are you?" Dylan looked up at Dante with wide innocent eyes and then he said the words that made my face burn as if I were standing directly under the sun. "Are you going to be my new daddy?"

 reorder Dante Here!

GET A FREE BOOK

Get A Free Book!

Join my mailing list to be informed of new releases and teasers and you will also receive a FREE Book!

ACKNOWLEDGMENTS

Special thanks go out to my proofreader, Marla Esposito, for always going above and beyond. Thank you for all your hard work.

I would also like to thank my beta readers Jo-Ann Forrest, Kim Green, Danielle Forgione, Sarah Ackerman, Michelle Manfre, Melissa Eiker, Nanette Cox, Kayla Berry, Mary Campbell, Stephanie Messier, Emily Kirkpatrick, Laci Danielle, Jackie Pinhorn, Kerri Long, Cilicia White, Trina McConnell, and Sarah Mathyssen for their feedback on the beginning of the book. Your encouragement and feedback was much appreciated.

And a huge thank you to all of my readers that have read and loved my books! There's nothing better than hearing from someone who has enjoyed one of my books.

CONNECT WITH J. S. COOPER

I love to hear from readers. You can email me at jscooper-author@gmail.com.

Connect with me on Instagram here.

Or follow me on Facebook here.

You can join my special J. S. Cooper VIP Group here!

51334151R00122

Made in the USA
Lexington, KY
02 September 2019